MW01147082

AFFLICTION

JENIKA SNOW

AFFLICTION

By Jenika Snow

www.JenikaSnow.com

Jenika_Snow@Yahoo.com

Copyright © April 2017 by Jenika Snow

First E-book Publication: April 2017

Photographer: Wander Aguiar :: Photography

Cover Model: Jonny James

Model image provided by: Wander Book Club

Cover created by: Popkitty

Editor: Kasi Alexander

Line Editor: Lea Ann Schafer

ALL RIGHTS RESERVED: The unauthorized reproduction, transmission, or distribution of any part of this copyrighted work is illegal. Criminal copyright infringement is investigated by the FBI and is punishable by up to 5 years in federal prison and a fine of $250,000.

This literary work is fiction. Any name, places, characters and incidents are the product of the author's imagination. Any resemblance to actual persons, living or dead, events or establishments is solely coincidental.

Please respect the author and do not participate in or encourage piracy of copyrighted materials that would violate the author's rights.

NEWSLETTER

Want to know when Jenika has book related news, and giveaways, and free books?

You can get all of that and more by following the link below!

————

Sign Up Here: http://eepurl.com/ce7yS-/

————

It wasn't until Cameron that I knew what real darkness was...or that I'd crave it so much.

I'd let the world weigh down on me, pull me under until nothing made sense anymore. Maybe that's how I let myself get into this mess. Maybe that's how I was in my current situation with a man I knew could save me from a fate worse than death. Even if being with Cameron, giving him every part of me, the only part that's worth anything—my body—might very well ruin me, I had to survive.

Drug lord. Crime boss. Murderer. I should fear him, be horrified by what he wanted from me, by who he was. But instead I found myself wanting to please him, wanting to give myself over completely.

Because I knew that gave me control over him.

Cameron Ashton reigned over the gritty underworld, the danger and violence of depravity, from his throne. A pistol is his sword, and apathy is his second-in-command. I knew he was dangerous, knew he'd break me and not think twice. But he was my only chance, the only way I'd survive.

And I didn't know how true that was until he owned me.

He's possessive and controlling. The darkness in him runs stronger, deeper than it ever has in me. Maybe we're not so different. Maybe giving up my control to Cameron, giving him my very soul, made me the powerful one?

Maybe, in the end, I'll be the one who owns him.

1

The sweat running down the valley between my breasts was like fingers moving along me. I was hot, my body flushed, my heart racing. Everything in me felt alive, ready to tear through my skin like another entity wanting to escape.

I was drunk, and I felt incredible.

The bodies pressed tightly against me, moving sexually, suggestively, made me feel even better. It made me feel alive. I moved with them, swaying to the music, inhaling the scent of sex and alcohol that seemed to surround me. I was sure a lot of people would be fucking tonight. No doubt it would be dirty, their inhibitions having been left at the club as they took home a random person. It would be the kind of sex that drunk people had, sloppy, carefree.

I wasn't a good girl.

I didn't even feel like the girl they called Sofia.

I didn't follow the rules. And my life was less than memorable. I lived like today was my last, because for all I knew it would be. It could be.

I came to this club when I couldn't stand the box that was my life, the one that was sealed tight, no airholes, no light getting through the crack. I got wasted, danced until my body was covered with sweat, my muscles sore, and some poor, hard-up frat guy got off in his jeans by grinding against my leg. I was a wreck in many ways, and I had no doubt that people assumed I was slutty by the way I dressed, by the way I moved on the dance floor.

But how I dressed and acted didn't make up who I was: a virgin who was lost, who had no one, nothing. I was an inexperienced woman who came here and danced because I wanted a little bit of release...the only kind I ever got. How I felt here was like being consumed by the water, of being helpless but weightless, of being sucked down to the very bottom where no light was permitted.

I wasn't light. I was darkness wrapped up in a five-foot-five frame, with dark hair, a wild streak, and no one to stop me.

Maybe I was a contradiction to myself, a lost girl who didn't know what she wanted in life. But it's who I was, how I got through each day.

I embraced it, knowing that maybe my upbringing, that having an absentee mother, a drunk for a father, and a penchant for getting slapped on occasion by said parents made me this way.

I wasn't broken, but I was damaged.

Or maybe it had nothing to do with my parents or what I didn't have growing up: love. Maybe I was just born this way.

Either way I didn't try and stop it. I didn't try and change.

"You look good out here dancing, girl." The feeling of a guy behind me, of his hands on my hips, his hard cock digging into my lower back, had dual sensations moving through me. "You feel good," he said again, his voice thick, aroused, slurred from the no doubt many drinks he'd consumed.

I wanted him to get off, because knowing I had that kind of control, that kind of power, fueled me. But on the other hand I felt disgust, mainly for myself. I felt and smelled his hot, liquor-laced breath along my neck. I shivered, and the way he groaned made me assume he thought it meant I was into this.

I wasn't, but I didn't stop from grinding on him.

I lifted my hands, closed my eyes, and just thought about something else. I wasn't here, wasn't trying to get this guy to come in his pants. I was far away, so distant that nothing could touch me.

"Come home with me. Hell, let's go back to my car."

I shook my head. He needed to shut up.

"Come on, girl." He ground his dick against me again. He felt small, even though he was hard.

"No. Either shut up and dance with me, or go find someone willing to go home with you." I didn't even know if he heard me over the rush of the music, but if he said one more word, I'd just go get a drink.

He tightened his hold on my hips, digging his small dick into my back. "I bet you're wet for me right now, aren't you?" His breath was hot, humid. It was acidic and I gagged.

I was bone-dry, not even the teasing of arousal playing over me. I never felt anything when I danced with these guys. It was what made me feel free, made me feel powerful in an otherwise unstable world. I might not have any kind of control with my personal life, with my finances, with anything that could ground me, but at this club, where the drinks flowed, the sex was potent, and my power was immense...I was the one in charge.

I'd been called a dick tease, a bitch, whore, a cunt... any and all of the above. None of that mattered. They were verbal bullets, and in this club I wore my bullet-proof vest.

I pushed away from the guy and made my way to the bar. He was either cursing me out or had hopefully moved on to someone more receptive to what he was actually after. But when I got to the bar, the people crammed together, shouting, lifting their hands to get one of the three bartenders to come their way. I decided tonight was done. I'd hit the bathroom, then call a cab.

Pushing my way through the throng of bodies, the air stale, humid, the heat suffocating, I said a silent prayer that the line to use the bathroom wasn't up the ass. But there were still a few girls ahead of me. I leaned against the wall, resting my head back on it, and stared up. I noticed the video camera aimed right at me. There were several in this hallway, two in the back, one pointing at me, and another aimed at the dance floor. I had no doubt there were a dozen more at other locations.

Although this place was wild on most nights, it also had a reputation for being safe—well, as safe as a nightclub could be. It had just been renovated by the new owner over the last year, a man I'd heard rumors about, and one I never wanted to meet.

Dark and dangerous. Violent and psychotic. He's not a person you want to meet in a dark alley. He'd just as soon slit your throat for looking at him the wrong way.

Rumors, of course, but it was those words, whispered by everyone and anyone, that told me there had to be a little bit of truth behind them.

I feel sorry for anyone who pisses off Cameron Ashton, because he'll solve that problem with a shovel and a six-foot-deep hole.

Pushing off the wall when it was my turn inside, I used the facility, went over to the sink to wash my hands, and stared at myself in the mirror. The girl who stared back looked sad, and not in an emotional way. My reflection showed a hot mess. My eyeliner was starting to smear under my eyes, pieces of my dark hair stuck to my temples, and the lipstick I had on, once red and vibrant, now looked dead and colorless.

I finished in the restroom, pushed my way through the crowd, and finally opened the door that led outside. The cool night air washed over me, and I involuntarily closed my eyes, moaning softly. It felt good out here, the crush of bodies and heat a distant memory the longer I stood here. The alcohol that had once numbed me, clouding my head with the nothingness, started to clear.

Maybe I hadn't been as drunk as I'd thought. Being behind those doors was like another world. The lights, music, the people trying to get off any way they could, brought you down low to a depraved, sticky and disgusting level. It's what I loved.

I needed to get home now, had work in the morning, had to get back to my shitty life. I fished my cell out of the miniscule handbag I carried with me, dialed the cab service I had memorized, and told them the address. Coming here for the last year should have had them knowing me by name. As I waited for them to arrive, ten long fucking minutes, I moved away from the front doors and leaned against the wall off to the side. I glanced up, the streetlight close by bright but not quite reaching me fully. Looking to my left, I noticed another security camera, this one pointed at the front doors. Never let it be said this place didn't have their shit together.

The sound of a lighter going off to my right had me glancing over. I saw the flare of the flame, smelled the scent of the cigarette as its owner inhaled and then exhaled.

"Hey, girl."

I exhaled. God, of course the guy from inside, the one with the small dick and the need for me to go home with him, would be out here. I didn't bother replying, didn't want to engage. Instead I turned my head in the other direction and glanced at a few people across the parking lot smoking. I felt the lightest touch on my arm.

The hell?

I glanced to my right, and before I knew what was happening, that light touch from the asshole turned into him pulling me farther into the shadowy side street.

2

"Hey," I shouted, but he clapped his hand over my mouth. Panic welled in me so violently I couldn't think straight. My heart started hammering against my ribs when he pushed me farther into the shadowy abyss.

He had me pinned to the side of the wall, the brick scraping along my back. There'd be marks on my flesh, but that was the least of my worries. His forearm on my throat cut off my oxygen. I clawed at his arm, my nails digging at his skin. He hissed and put more pressure on my neck. My head started to grow fuzzy, my body going numb. I was far beyond panicking, the survival instinct rising up violently.

"You stupid fucking cunt," he said close to my face, his breath smelling stale, the aroma of the cigarette he'd been smoking making me sick to my stomach. I might have thrown up if I hadn't been struggling to breathe

The sound of a belt buckle being undone, of a zipper being pulled down, brought reality crashing down on me. I wouldn't be able to get out of this, not without a hell of a lot more damage than just the scrapes on my back. The sound of people coming in and out of the club was so close, yet so far away.

"You should have taken me up on my offer to come back to my place. I would have been gentle with you."

Lies.

"But now you'll get fucked in this dirty alley like the whore you are."

I felt his erection against my belly. I tried to say something, to yell out, do anything that would make me more than a victim waiting to get attacked.

The flash of headlights pulling into the alley had my attacker stilling and glancing to the side. He kept his forearm on my throat but tucked himself back into his pants. He moved closer to me so I had no doubt that whoever was in that car couldn't see his arm pressing into me, cutting off my oxygen. It was clear he didn't care or was too drunk to have a problem with someone seeing us in this position. But I supposed it might look like two people about to get it on...both consenting, even though I wanted to knee this fucker in the balls.

"Make one sound and I'll find out where you live,

come in through your window, and really do some damage."

God, was the frat-boy appearance just a cover for his psychotic nature? But no way in hell I'd take his threat seriously, even if he meant one word. This would be my only chance to get help. Because even if I did nothing, he'd still destroy me.

The car was a good ten feet away, the headlights shining right on us, the vehicle just idling now. It seemed like forever before the sound of a door opening and closing came louder than the rush of conversation from the club goers just around the corner. And then I heard feet hitting pavement in an easy, relaxed pace; then the sight of a large body—very large—came into view. I could only assume it was a man, given the size. He stayed behind the lights, the shadows wrapping around his tall frame.

He stared at us for long seconds, and for some reason all I could do was stare right back. I started to struggle. I caught the asshole holding me off guard and managed to push him back enough that his forearm was no longer pressed painfully into my throat. I sucked in oxygen, sweet, life-sustaining oxygen. My throat burned, and a flush stole over me, the pain of being able to breathe again claiming me.

"You fucking bitch," the asshole next to me hissed.

And then there was the sound of another door opening and closing, of a gun being cocked. The shadowy man tipped his head to the side. It was the slightest move, but it caused whoever had just gotten out of the car to start walking toward us.

"The fuck?" the asshole pinned against me said in a hushed voice, his eyes squinted, the headlights blinding us. I feared the worst, thinking maybe I'd misjudged whoever had shown up as being able to help. Maybe they were worse than the fucker who'd attacked me.

And then the guy was pulled away from me, the sweet relief of his body no longer on mine urging me to run. But I was frozen in place, the dark shapes still covered in the shadows, the headlights still blinding me, making it impossible to see anything clearly. I rubbed my throat, the burn almost unbearable.

And then a body was thrown against the side of the building, and I realized it was the would-be frat boy. I stood there shocked, unable to move, as I watched a man approach. He was in front of the car, his body illuminated by the intense yellow glow of his headlights. But his face was still concealed. An air of danger came from this man like a punch to my gut. I sucked in more oxygen, this time not having anything to do with the fact I was struggling to breathe.

I stared at the man currently holding the asshole up against the brick wall by his neck. Whoever the man was, he was big, supporting another human as if it was nothing at all. I covered my chest, despite the fact that I was dressed. I was bared, like I was so open my secrets were exposed. When I glanced at the man who'd tilted his head, who'd sent his guard dog to do his bidding, I could feel his gaze on me. I might not be able to see his face, but I felt his eyes on me like fingers touching me, stroking me, holding me down.

And then my heart seized in my chest as I watched him lift his arm, the gun I'd heard being cocked most likely the one he held. He took a step closer, not to me, but to the body pinned to the wall. The guy was struggling to breathe, clawing at the grip the man had on his throat.

Just like me. A taste of his own medicine.

He kept moving closer to the man pinned to the wall, but I knew he watched me, knew he was calculating all of this. I thought I'd be able to see him when he moved away from the headlights. But once he was standing next to his partner or guard dog or whatever the hell the guy was to him, I still couldn't make out his face. I knew I wouldn't have known him anyway, but I wanted to look into the face of the man who'd saved me.

Saved me?

Yes, he'd saved me from a very dark hole, pulled me out so I could breathe again. But I now had this feeling, this sensation like honey on my skin, thick, almost suffocating me again, that this man was far more dangerous than anything I'd ever come across.

He said nothing, and the only sound that penetrated my foggy brain was of the man struggling, of his wheezes and gasps as he tried to claw at the hand holding him, keeping him up. I felt nothing, no sympathy for him, nothing but the need to see him hurt the way he'd hurt me. And then, my lungs clenching painfully with every inhalation I made, I watched the man push away his partner and take his place in front of Frat Boy. Instinct, survival told me to run, to get the hell out of here because this was going straight into hell, where the flames licked at me, threatening to burn me alive.

The man had his head turned in my direction, the fucking shadows making him seem almost unreal, like maybe this was all a hallucination. He was so big, taller, thicker, and more muscular than the man pressed to the wall in front of him. Still he stayed silent; still he watched me. And then he lifted his hand, placed the barrel of the gun against my attacker's forehead, right in the damn center, and everything seemed to stand still. I knew enough about guns, had seen plenty of movies, to know the silencer attached would make this clean, would have no one panicking and rushing away at the sound of a gunshot.

I took a step forward, not sure why I'd do that. It was the equivalent of trying to touch a chained, starved dog, wanting to run my hands over it even though I knew it would attack me, tear me from limb to limb.

"No," I said. He might have been about to attack me, rape me, God, who knew what else. I couldn't stand here and watch some man shoot him. I didn't want that hanging over me, even if he deserved that and more. "I don't want that," I whispered. A long moment passed, maybe a second, maybe an hour. It seemed like ages where my body was stiff, my heart thundering, the man with the gun staring at me. He didn't pull the trigger, even though maybe he should have. I felt dizzy, my head swimming, the feeling of falling having nothing to do with the drinks I'd had or the situation that had transpired up until right now. "It's not worth it. He's not worth it," I whispered again, but even though I didn't know this man, I knew that he wasn't the type to give a shit about what was worth it or not. He did what he did because he wanted to.

I knew that as well as I knew the man with the gun pointed to his head could be shot dead at any second.

I was very aware of the blood rushing through my veins, drowning everything else out. The frat guy was saying something, but I couldn't hear it, couldn't focus on anything but the man in front of me who held so much power it could have brought me to my knees.

After a tense second he took a step back, the gun still in his hand, his focus now on the asshole who'd had me in a choke hold. He still hadn't said one word, not when he cocked the weapon, and not when he had his thug slam the frat-guy up against the building. And he didn't say anything when he lifted his arm and rammed the butt of the gun at the asshole's temple. The guy slid to the ground, maybe knocked out, maybe trying to make himself smaller, less noticeable.

And then there was nothing but him and me, staring at each other, the air thick, the world washing away. He turned and left me standing there, his hand at his side, the gun still in his grasp. The flash of a ring caught my attention, a thick one wrapped around his pinky, seeming much more ominous than it should. He got back in the car and drove off. I followed the car with my gaze, watching it disappear down the road, knowing he was staring at me the same as I was him.

I had no idea what in the hell had happened.

I didn't know if I'd ever be the same.

3

I wiped the sleep from my eyes, my dreams from last night consisting of a big, dark man. Even though I couldn't see his face, I knew he was more dangerous than anything I could have come up against. He'd had ropes around me, laughing in this deep, sick, and twisted way that had made my humanity run and bury itself deep inside of me.

I'd slept for shit because of it. The dreams coupled with what I'd witnessed last night had been enough to keep me up, a warm glass of tea in my hand...the only thing stable enough to tie me to reality in that moment.

"Darryl's got your check in back," Rita, the assistant manager of this shitty coffee shop, said as she passed me.

"Thanks," I mumbled. I had bills stacked against each other back in my shitty apartment, and although I worked overtime, I still wasn't making it, was still struggling just to survive.

The story of my life.

I finished tying on my apron and walked over to Darryl's office. My pervert of a boss was hunched over his desk, his cell pressed up to his ear as he barked into the receiver.

"I don't care what he said. I asked him to be here an hour ago." A moment of silence passed before he spoke again. "Listen, if he doesn't show up, then I'll give his position to someone else." He disconnected the call and tossed the phone. I stood there for a second before clearing my throat. Darryl turned and looked at me.

Okay, he's not in a pervert mood, not when he's mean mugging me like that.

I'd take his anger over him slipping in lewd comments any day.

"Rita said my check was here?"

He started pushing papers aside until he got to the stack of envelopes. After flipping through them and finally finding mine, he handed it over without looking at me.

"Can you come in tomorrow an hour early?" he said, still not looking at me. He was such a shitty fucking boss.

"Yeah." I needed the extra money, needed another job really. As it was, working at the coffee shop wasn't cutting it. My electric was going to get cut off any day, and I was barely scraping by enough to pay my rent.

Cutting out the bar scene is going to have to be a priority.

I hated myself on some level for going out at all, for spending what little money I had. But if I didn't get out, I'd kill myself. Maybe not literally, but I'd be stuck in that shitty apartment, no heat or electricity, staring at the wall. I'd be waiting for the world to swallow me up, because that would have been the only thing I had going for me.

"Actually, I was wondering if you had any overtime?"

He looked at me then and shook his head. Man, he had a bug up his ass big-time today, but I'd take it over his wandering eyes and his crude comments.

"Sorry, I'm strapped for hours. What you are scheduled is all you're getting." And that was it. He waved at me to leave, and I forced myself not to make an under the breath comment.

Asshole.

I got to work because thinking about my problems, about the fact I'd have to find another job, wasn't what I wanted to dwell on. I had no one to ask for help, no one that really gave a damn about me. I was on my own in every possible way.

Twenty-two years old and a shell of a woman, an empty vessel that has nothing good going for her.

I shouldn't have had to feel alive by clubbing and getting drunk. I should have had some light and happiness in my world. But then I knew that wasn't how reality worked.

I SAT on the curb at the back of the coffee shop. I had three more hours before my shift was over with, before I'd go back to the crushing realization of where I actually was in this world. It was times like this where the stress was almost too much to handle, where it tightened its hold on my lungs, squeezing me, trying to make me go blue and wither away into nothing, that I wished I had a cigarette. They were vile things, but smoking would have given me a small out, a tiny thing to focus on as the world went upside down around me.

The sound of the door opening had me glancing back. Marshall came through, a white trash bag in his hand, his ball cap crooked. He looked just as worn-out on the outside as I felt on the inside.

"Hey," he said, his smile genuine.

"Hey." I focused on the back of the building in front of me. It was an antique shop. Maybe they were hiring? I felt someone close by, watching me, and looked over to see Marshall staring at me. "What's up?"

"I heard you talking to Darryl about needing extra hours."

I nodded, not sure where this was going. Marshall was lower on the totem pole than I was, and he barely worked as it was.

He looked around as if he was afraid, as if he didn't

want anyone overhearing. Then he came closer, the smell of coffee beans coming from him in the same strength I assumed it came from me.

"You're really hard up for money?" He was sitting beside me on the curb now, and I could see how his eyes were a little bloodshot, his pupils a little dilated. He seemed jumpy, but by the way he acted I could assume he was just nervous.

Or juiced up on something.

"I mean, I guess," I said, my eyebrows pulled down, my confusion strong.

He was silent for long seconds, fidgeting with his apron, looking nervous as hell. "I know a guy who can help."

"That doesn't sound ominous at all."

He kept looking around, and I felt the hairs on my arms stand on end. "I think I'll pass on whatever it is you're offering."

"Sorry," he said and exhaled. "But I do know someone who can help. He helps a lot of people."

"Yeah, out of the kindness of his heart I assume."

Marshall shrugged. "Here." He reached in his apron and grabbed a pen and piece of paper. He wrote down an address, then handed it to me.

I glanced down at it, not sure where this part of the city was. "Thanks?" I said, because this seemed pretty shifty.

"But seriously, he can help." Marshall stood and headed back inside. I should have tossed the address, because no way in hell this sounded legit or even safe. But for some reason I put it in my apron and stood.

What I knew for sure was nothing was free.

4

I could barely keep my eyes open as I drove my shitty car back to my shittier apartment. I took the last right onto the street, saw the apartment building looming up ahead, and parked right at the curb. For a second I just sat there, listening to the engine cooling, that clicking. I did this every day when I came home, dreading going in there, hating that I'd be alone.

No real friends.

No family that gave a shit about me.

One day a month where I let loose, where I pretended to be someone else.

That was my life summed up.

I stopped feeling sorry for myself and headed inside. The elevator was broken, had been for the last month. I doubted it would get fixed anytime soon, not unless a bunch of people complained. Which they wouldn't, because anyone who lived here didn't really care about anything.

The first two flights of stairs were easy, the third and fourth made me realize I was out of shape. Thighs burning, lungs seizing, I adjusted my messenger bag and took the last step. My head was downcast, my focus on the dirty ground with the cracked and peeling linoleum. When I lifted my head, the first thing I saw was my apartment door cracked open. My heart stalled. I'd locked it. I knew I had. This was a bad neighborhood, and although I didn't have shit worth a grain of salt in there, having someone break in was an invasion.

I should have called the cops, but again this was a bad neighborhood, and even if the cops did come by, it would take forever, and they'd assume I just didn't lock the door.

I had my keys in my hand, the metal sticking out between my fingers. I'd use it as a weapon if I had to. Creeping slowly toward the door, I pushed it open with my shoe. I could have maybe asked one of my neighbors to come with me, but with them being drunks, junkies, or senile, I didn't think they would be much help. Besides, everyone here kept to themselves and didn't worry about others...it was usually safer that way.

The door swung open, and I saw that my place had been trashed. It hadn't been a looker to begin with, and I really had nothing of value...expect my coffee can. My heart started beating a static rhythm. I shut the door, my safety not coming into play at this moment as I rushed to the kitchen. The cupboards were all open, the few dishes I had crashed to the floor. And there, among the shards of thrift-store ceramic, was my coffee can. It was on its side, the lid a foot away. I knew it would be empty even before I picked it up with a shaking hand.

I'd been saving any little amount of money from my paychecks, putting a dollar in the can here or there, or a few quarters. It was sometimes my free-for-one-day-a-month fund, what I'd dip into to buy a few drinks if I had any extra. Hell, I used it to put gas in my car when money was really tight.

I sat on the floor, my legs feeling like they'd give out, my heart in my throat. The sadness was soon replaced with anger. I cried, hating that I couldn't do better, knowing I deserved better. I tossed that fucking coffee can across the kitchen, the metal slamming against the cupboard. Then I put my head in my hands and cried, just bawled because there was nothing else to do. Maybe I didn't have that much money in the coffee can anyway. Maybe I shouldn't have even had money around, or hid it better.

Maybe. Maybe. Maybe.

There were a lot of things I could have, should have done differently. In the end, my life was still the same, still broken, twisted and gnarled, with the light I thought I needed drifting further away. Maybe I wasn't supposed to have that light. Maybe I only deserved the darkness.

Maybe that's what made me stronger.

I lifted my head, wiped the tears away angrily, and realized what I had in my pocket. I pulled that slip of paper out, the address scribbled across it seeming so damn ominous. Everything in me screamed to throw it away, but the reality of my situation was I was falling deeper into a hole. I just needed to get on my feet, find a second job, and then I could look for something better for myself, something that wasn't infested with hatred and anger.

My hand was still shaking when I shoved the paper back into my pocket. I stood, held my keys tighter, and headed out the door. I didn't bother locking it this time. Because what was the point?

———

I PULLED my car to a stop, leaned forward, and stared up at the building. It looked abandoned, decay and age written all over it. Glancing at the piece of paper again, I knew this was the right place, but it looked fucked up for sure.

This is stupid. Get the fuck out of here.

About to do just that, because I'd rather scrape by than end up dead, I went to pull away. The sound of someone pounding on the hood of my car had a startled cry leaving me. The man in front of the car was wearing a hood and a dark mask that only covered half of his face. He took a step back, my headlights illuminating him. He was dressed head to toe in black, his body still in front of my vehicle. I could have mowed him down if I'd really wanted to get the hell out of there, which I did. But the truth was I was scared shitless. And I knew he wasn't alone.

The sound of banging at the back of my car had my heart racing so hard it was painful.

"Turn the car off." The deep voice beside my car had me jumping. When I didn't move, he held up a gun, tapping the barrel on the glass of my driver's side window. "Move it," he shouted.

I turned the key, shutting the car off. It felt like I'd unplugged my lifeline.

"Get out of the fucking car."

I was too scared to try and make a run for it, the images of bullets flying through my car and slamming into me playing like a grotesque movie reel in my head.

I was out of the car faster than I thought I could move, and instantly pushed up against the side of the vehicle, the metal cold, hard, and unforgiving. The guy keeping me flat on the car started patting me down like I was packing a weapon. Surely they could see how terrified I was. I was spun around so fast my head swam. This guy was wearing the same mask, his eyes shrewd, dark.

"What the fuck are you doing here?"

"I...I..." My mouth wouldn't work, the words not coming out, not being formed properly.

"Speak up, you fucking bitch, or I'll really give you

something to stutter about." He placed the barrel of the gun at my abdomen, pressing it in, showing me who was in charge.

"Marshall gave me the address, said a man could help me." The words tumbled out of my mouth, and I was proud and terrified I'd spoken them. I could hear how scared I sounded. I was scared, shaking, my nails digging into my palms. I was surprised there wasn't blood on my hands, a testament to the violence swirling in the air. I glanced around. Four men, all of them dressed the same.

Thugs.

"People need to learn to keep their mouths shut."

He's referring to Marshall. God, I shouldn't have said anything, shouldn't have named him. I was so scared.

Before I knew what was happening, I was being hauled away from the car and toward the building. I tripped over my feet, but the guy holding on to my arm squeezed tighter. I wasn't foolish enough to think he would care if I fell on my face.

We entered the building through this rusted-as-hell door. One of the guys hung outside, and the other three all but pushed me inside. The stench of dirt and mold was almost unbearable, and I coughed. Was that why they wore the masks? Or was it to make people like me know how low I was to them, how dangerous they really were?

I was pushed through a set of doors, then pulled down a long hallway. Another door. Another hallway. I felt like we'd been walking forever, going deeper, the chill in the air becoming more intense. Finally we pushed through a door, and I could see tables all around. Guns and drugs littered the tables.

It was then I knew that there was no going back. They'd let me see this, and although I didn't know what their faces looked like, I knew where they holed up.

"Ricky, yo, we got a live one here." The man holding my arm finally let go. He pushed me forward, and I stumbled again, catching myself on a table covered in large square-shaped bags wrapped in duct tape.

I glanced up at the one named Ricky, my throat dry, tight. I expected him to have the same getup as his thugs, but he was wearing dirty jeans, an equally filthy shirt, and sporting greasy hair. He had a cigarette hanging from his too-thin lips, and he eyed me up and down. I felt naked in that moment.

God, what have I gotten myself into?

5

"Y ou're scaring her. Ease up," Ricky said to the guys behind me. And although he might be trying to make me calm, his too-pleasant voice and the way he smiled made my skin crawl.

I straightened, clutching my hands to my stomach. I knew it was a defensive move, probably making me seem weaker.

"What's your name?"

I had a feeling lying to this guy wouldn't do me any good. Hell, I'd left my bag in the car, and I was sure they'd already rummaged through it, seeing my driver's license, where I lived.

"Sofia." I only gave him my first name, hoping he didn't press for anything else.

"How did you find out about this place, about me?"

I rubbed my hands on my jeans and glanced behind me at the three guys. When I faced Ricky again, I realized he'd moved closer. "I got your name and address from a guy I know."

He cocked his head. "A guy you know?"

"Marshall," one of the thugs said.

"Marshall has a big mouth," Ricky said, still eyeing me, making me feel dirty with the way he looked at me. "But that's what you get with a junkie."

"I...I don't think I should be here." The words came from me before I could stop them. I knew better than to think they'd just let me go.

"Calm down," he said, moving closer. I couldn't move, though, and even if I could, I knew there wouldn't be anywhere for me to run to. "You clearly need something, and I'm here to help." He held out his arms, his ego grand. "Tell me, Sofia, what do you need from me?" There he went, looking me up and down, making me want to go take a shower, wash off his presence. "Go on, tell me. You're wasting precious time here."

"No, I don't think I need anything."

"Fucking tell me what you need." He slammed his fist down on the table, causing one of the duct-taped squares to roll off another. I jumped, my heart racing, the sound filling my head.

"I came here for money." This man was crazy. I could

see it on his face, in the way his eyes shifted back and forth. He smelled like booze and cigarettes, sweat and degradation.

He grinned, and it was an ugly sight. "Money? I can help you with that." He gestured me closer, and although I wanted to run out of there, I wasn't a total moron. They'd catch me, and I nearly vomited at the thought of what they would do to me.

I took a step closer, my throat so dry, my mind rushing with what I could do to get out of here. He took me to one of the tables off to the back, where I saw piles of cash. Some were in bundles wrapped with plastic, while others were clearly in the process of being counted. He took a stack and handed it to me. I didn't take it, my limbs feeling like lead, fear too strong in me to even move.

"Go on, take it," he said, his face almost jovial. I shook my head, an act I didn't even know I was doing until it was done. His face hardened. "You're going to come to my place of business, asking for help, and then refuse what I offer?" God, he was insane, his shifty-as-hell eyes looking at me, checking me out. He was probably thinking some pretty disgusting thoughts.

"I...I couldn't pay you back, not that much." I stared at the stack of money. It could easily get me out of the hole I was in, but that was not something I could repay, not in this lifetime.

He shrugged. "We can work something out." He looked at my breasts, and the need to cover myself, despite being fully clothed, rode me hard.

"Actually, I've changed my mind. Thank you for the offer, but I'll just go." I started to back up, but the feeling of a hard body behind me made me stop. I didn't have to turn around to know it was one of his masked men.

Ricky took a step forward. He was so close now that the disgusting scent of him washed over me. "No, you'll take this, because you're already here." He grinned, revealing crooked, yellowing teeth. "Because if you don't take it, Sofia," he said, lifting his gaze to mine, "if you don't take this money, I can't let you go." He tipped his head to the side. "You understand what I'm saying?"

You've already seen us. You already know where we do our illegal shit. If you go, we'll have to kill you.

"I understand," I said, my voice threadbare. But I straightened my shoulders, not wanting to appear weak. That would make them attack like a pack of wild hyenas.

"Good," Ricky said and all but shoved the money at me. "We can work out payment details later." He eyed me again, that disgusting smile on his face. "In the meantime, don't try and run, because Bobbie boy got all your information from your ID."

I turned and looked over my shoulder. One of the masked men held up my purse. Yeah, I'd assumed they'd go through my shit. "And if I can't pay you back?" I asked, trying to keep my voice calm, collected.

Ricky's grin faded, and he got this crazed look in his eyes—even more than what was already going on. "Everyone ends up paying one way or another. We always find a way."

6

Several days later

I had no intentions of spending this money, not when my life was going to be the collateral if I couldn't repay it.

I stared at the stack, that wad of cash sitting on my shitty table like a lead weight. I could have said I didn't want it, tried to make a run for it, but I wasn't foolish enough to think I would have made it out of there alive.

"You stupid girl." I rested my head in my hands, the tears threatening to come out, but my self-hatred made everything else stand down. But for as stupid as I was for even going there, and allowing my emotions at this horrible time to consume me, I also knew just giving back the money wasn't enough. They'd want interest, and whatever that interest was had never been discussed.

I grabbed the money, went over to the sink, and bent down. Behind the pipes was a loose piece of wall. After popping it off, I shoved the cash back there. I had just found the "secret" space earlier in the week, and even though I hadn't known about it before, I cursed myself for not putting the damn coffee can there to begin with. Once I shoved the few decades-old cleaning supplies out of the way to make it not look obvious I had been messing around under the sink, I got up and headed to work. I didn't know how much worse this situation could get, but I had a feeling it wouldn't get any easier.

"Does anyone know where Marshall is, or has anyone heard from him?" Silence greeted Rita, the lead for the day. "He hasn't been to work in three days, and I can't get ahold of him."

My heart started beating faster. I hadn't seen him since that day he gave me Ricky's address. And although I could have said I was overreacting, something deep inside of me said I'd been the one to cause his disappearance.

I started sweating, beads forming between my breasts, along my spine.

"Well, if anyone speaks with him, tell him he's out. He's been fired. We can only handle so many no-call and no-shows."

My heart was thundering hard now, and as I watched Rita leave, I knew I was to blame. If anything had happened to Marshall, it was because of me. I'd opened my mouth, and now he hadn't been to work. I had to see him, to make sure he was okay at the very least. I had know that my foolishness and big mouth hadn't killed him. I might not have known him very well, but he didn't deserve to die.

I finished out the workday, my mind jumbled, a mess, threads of worry, confusion, and fear for my own safety weighing on me. The image of that money sitting on my table, and the implications of it all was a heavy weight, making the panic rise to a blistering level.

I fished my car keys out of my purse, waited until I saw Rita leave to go up front, and slipped into the manager's office. With the coffee shop still running on actual employee files instead of them being on the computer, I was able to find Marshall's address easily enough.

Once I was in my car and heading toward his place, I felt my heart thunder. My chest ached, the reality of my life and where I was right now making me sick to my stomach. When I pulled up to Marshall's housing unit, I held on to my steering wheel even harder. He lived in a shittier neighborhood than I did. The sound of sirens in the distance was barely discernible. What I did hear was men shouting, crude language being thrown around, and glass shattering.

Before I could talk myself into just leaving, because I didn't want to be put in an even crazier situation, the front door opened and a woman who looked worse for wear came out. She had shorts on high enough they left nothing to the imagination. Her legs had bruises on them, and her shirt was a piece of fabric barely covering her large breasts. Her hair was a rat's nest atop her head, the black roots coming out an inch before her bleach-blonde hair. I could see the track marks easily enough on the insides of her elbows, but I grabbed on to my courage and reached over to roll down the window.

"Excuse me?"

She glanced over at me but quickly looked away and kept walking.

"Excuse me? I'm looking for someone."

"If you're smart, a pretty girl like you would get the fuck out of here." She glanced at me once more, a black eye now visible under the washed-out streetlamp.

I rolled up the window, making sure the doors were locked. There was one second where panic settled deep in me. My throat closed up, and my heart started to make this warlike tempo in my chest, the pain strangulating.

I closed my eyes, gripped the steering wheel, and tried to breathe through the fear. When I opened my eyes, I was exactly where I had been five seconds ago.

There was a flash of headlights, and I glanced in my rearview mirror, seeing a shiny dark SUV pull up behind me. That panic grew tenfold. It was probably nothing, or maybe it was something. Didn't know, but what I did know without a doubt was that if I didn't figure out what in the hell I was going to do, I'd be dead.

7

My mind was filled with white noise, this static that consumed me. I stared down at the empty coffee cup, the insulated Styrofoam fragile in my hand. Before I knew what I was doing, I had it crushed in my palm, my fingers digging into the slightly raised exterior.

"Excuse me?"

I lifted my head, feeling like there was this rush of waves around me, filling my ears, making noise muted, blurred. The lady in front of me had this confused look on her face, or maybe it was fear. She looked at me like I'd grown two heads.

"Are you going to make my coffee?"

I swallowed, my hands shaking. Why the hell was I even at work?

"Take fifteen," Cambria said, pushing me toward

the back.

I blinked, my vision blurry. I was crying.

I found myself walking into the room, stopping, standing there, looking around but not taking anything in. I felt lost, so lost my mind was a jumble of images and words, sounds of what happened around me. But just as promptly I turned and went out of the back room and right to a table.

I sat in one of the empty booths, wanting to leave, to get away from all of this, from everything, but I needed the money.

God, I could have laughed at that fact. I had a shitload of money back at my apartment, but still I was broke, wondering how I would survive.

I scrubbed my hand over my face, over my hair, wanting to rip the strands out. At least the pain would have given me something else to focus on. The flat screen that hung in the corner showed the news. That's all that was on, every day, all day. I stared at the muted screen, the news anchor saying something, but the volume was so low I couldn't hear anything. I watched her mouth move, stared at her perfectly placed and made-up face, and wanted to scream. I was frustrated, my mind and body feeling like it was wrapped around itself, like it was this tangled mess inside of me with no hope of becoming right again.

And then the screen switched to a neighborhood, one I recognized because I'd just been there the other day. I sat up straighter, staring at the shitty complex where Marshall lived. The apartment building was the focal point, and the people standing around were more interested in the fact that a camera was there than the body that was being wheeled out on a stretcher. I obviously couldn't see who they were taking away, but I didn't need to see to know it was Marshall. The image of him flashed on the screen. The news anchor was back on, the little square to the upper-right side of her showing the guy I didn't really know, but who I felt responsible for at this moment.

He looked lost in the picture, his eyes red-rimmed, his face ashen. His death had to be something vicious, something truly newsworthy if they were taking time to report on it. Hell, his neighborhood probably had a high violence and death rate, so whatever had happened to Marshall had to be pretty bad for them to give it the time of day.

I'd killed him. He'd told me about Ricky, tried to help me, and because I'd opened my mouth, his death was on my hands. I found myself standing, went over to where the TV was mounted, and craned my neck back. I stared at the picture of him, everything moving in slow motion, the world around me spinning, then promptly speeding up.

I don't know what made me look out the window, but before I knew what I was doing, I stared out at the passing world before me. The only thing separating me from it was glass and steel. There, sitting like an idling devil, or maybe the Grim Reaper, was a black SUV. *The black SUV I'd seen at Marshall's place.*

I couldn't see who sat in the passenger's or driver's seat; the windows were too tinted, too dark with violence and death. But I knew they were there for me. I knew they were there to incite fear, promise.

I had to decide what I was going to do. Now.

———

THE MUSIC FILLED MY HEAD, the crush of bodies, the heat...all of it had this calm settling over me. Maybe I was a fool, an idiot for coming to the club, for not locking myself up, trying to hide, maybe even escaping the city. But all these people made me feel safer. These strangers made me feel like I was already hidden, a dot of color in the middle of a rainbow.

I didn't need to see Ricky to know he was in that dark SUV, that he was watching me, waiting for me to do something, anything that would give him an excuse to react. Or maybe he was just taunting me, torturing me with the promise of what my future really held.

I stood in the center of the room and turned around slowly, taking in the sights and smells that surrounded me. I felt like I could hide in plain sight, like nothing could touch me. There was strength in numbers, right?

Stupid. None of these assholes would look your way if you

needed help.

I closed my eyes and breathed in and out slowly. Sweat, stale beer, the promise of sex in the air, all of it filled my head, made me dizzy. The music was loud, the vibrations settling into my body, twisting me up, making me sway like I was in the ocean and the current was trying to take me under, to make me its bitch. I had no money on me, couldn't even get a drink to numb my emotions. I could have gone to the trouble of asking some poor asshole here to buy me a drink, ply him with the false promise of sex for a bottle of beer, but even that seemed like too much work. Just being here, the crush of bodies making me move back and forth, was enough to placate me.

It was enough to make me feel a modicum of safety.

Up until I step out of these doors and am forced to go back to my shitty apartment.

"Dance with me." The voice came through like a whip to my back. I didn't even turn around, didn't even look at whoever was offering his company. I just pushed my way through and walked toward the bar.

There were people milling around, throwing out their drink orders. The three bartenders worked fast, concentration etched on their faces. I glanced up to where several security cameras pointed to the patrons, taking in every little move, every hand being lifted. Who was on the other end? Who watched everyone from the safety of a padded chair and an eagle eye?

Did I even care?

"Let me buy you a drink."

I glanced to my left, my head feeling like it weighed a ton as I turned it. The guy sitting next to me looked nice, with a light gray button-down shirt, his tie loosened and his hair slicked off to the side. He was clearly a businessman, maybe coming to the club to unwind after a stressful day of mergers. I looked down at his hand, saw the gold wedding band, and lifted my gaze back to his face. He didn't look the least bit ashamed that he was here, trying to pick up some random girl while his wife was probably at home with his kids.

I didn't even bother responding. Being here wasn't helping me, not like I'd hoped. I'd wanted to be surrounded by people, to feel like I was nothing among a sea of everything. Instead I felt suffocated, like my own thoughts, my own needs were taking me further into the recesses of a place I'd never be able to claw myself back up from.

But going "home" wasn't an option. I needed fresh air, needed to breathe. I needed to still be close enough to something, to someone instead of surrounded by nothing. I pushed my way past the deadbeat husband, through the heavy crush of bodies gyrating on the dance floor, and finally made it outside. I sucked in a deep lungful of air. A few people were smoking to the side, the stench of cigarette smoke cloying, suffocating. I moved past them, turned the corner of the building, and found myself in a semi-quiet, pretty dark alley.

I had some privacy, some breathing room, but stayed close enough to the corner of the building to feel like I wasn't alone and foolish for coming out here. When I sat on the curb, the smell of piss, vomit, and stale beer filled my head, making me want to gag. But I didn't move. I felt this tingle of reality deep inside me, this problem that I'd never solve making me its prisoner. I could hear people around the corner, their laughter, their drunkenness causing them to be carefree.

I stared at the alleyway before me, the darkness creeping around, promising absolution, nothingness. That's what I wanted, to just be swallowed whole.

This alley wasn't where my problems stemmed from, just the one where the mystery man had taken control and "saved" me with a gun and unconcern. No, my problems had started when I was born into a world that didn't want me, when I was introduced into a life that already hated me.

I looked up and into the "eye" of the security camera pointed at me.

I pushed the tears away with angry swipes to my cheeks. I wouldn't cry for anything, for anyone, least of all myself. I'd gotten into this mess, and I'd figure out a way to get out of it.

Leaving. Running. That was my only option. They might find me, probably would if I was being honest, but they'd just take me here, now, anyway. Running would at least not make me a victim. It would make me a fighter, and that's how I'd survive.

Until they catch up with me, which they will eventually.

I scrubbed a hand over my face, so tired. I hung my head, closed my eyes, and just let the deep bass of the music come through whenever the front door was opened. The hairs on the back of my neck suddenly stood on end. I lifted my head and saw large black boots in my vision. I couldn't see the man who stood in front of me clearly, the shadows were too thick, but for some inexplicable reason I knew I'd seen him before.

That night in the alley. He was with the man in the suit.

They'd been dangerous, the violence swirling around them like an imprint, a promise. They hadn't said one word, yet their message had come through loud and clear.

And then he held his hand out to me. I should have gotten up and left. I didn't need any more trouble, but I found myself just sitting there, looking at it, wondering if it was a lifeline or an offer to drag me further into hell.

"He wants to see you," the man said, his voice deep, serrated. I felt his words slice into me like a rusty knife, opening me up, draining me dry.

But instead of going, leaving the clear threat I knew awaited me, I found myself placing my hand in his, letting him lift me off the ground, and following him as he led me farther into the darkness.

8

As soon as I stepped through the door I knew exactly where I was, who sat in front of me. I didn't know his name, but I knew he was the man who'd been in the alley, the one who'd pistol-whipped that asshole who'd assaulted me.

His office was hot, or maybe it was the way he stared at me. It was like he could see right into my very soul, and threatened to snatch it up and devour it if things didn't go his way.

He didn't say anything for long seconds, but his silence spoke volumes. "Come closer," he said—ordered —calmly.

I took a step forward.

"You know who I am?"

I shook my head. "I mean—" I swallowed after I said

those two words. "You're the man from the alley, the one who saved me."

"Saved you?" He leaned back in his chair, his focus on me.

I nodded. "From that asshole." I stared at the TV monitors behind him, an array of shots of the interior and exterior of the club. He was the one behind the "eye" then, watching, calculating.

I heard the door behind me shut with a deafening, final *click*. I was now left alone with this man.

I'd been a crying mess, broken and so damn scared of where my life was going, when that other shoe would drop, I hadn't even been able to stand. But here I was, for some unknown reason, and I didn't know whether to beg for help or run in the other direction.

I felt like I was this little rabbit facing a feral, starved lion.

I had no doubt I'd find out soon enough. My heart raced, my head swam with the realization that this was bad, and that I'd put myself in a dangerous situation. Coming here hadn't been smart; I felt that as strongly as I felt my heart pounding in my chest.

I'm already in a dangerous situation, one that will get me killed...or worse.

It was that "or worse" that scared the shit out of me. It was the image of being tied up, beaten, bloody, naked, my body a vessel for men who wanted nothing more than to empty themselves in me. Hell, I didn't know for sure he'd even do any of that to me, but I wasn't a fool either, despite my actions.

But this man in front of me seemed different, more calculating, and more dangerous.

"I'm Cameron Ashton," he said, his head now cocked to the side, his gaze taking me in as if he could see into the very depths of my soul. "You really have no idea who I am, despite coming to my club all this time." He didn't phrase it like a question.

I just shook my head.

I stared at the monitors again, reality and relaxation settling in. "You've been watching me?" I whispered those words, knowing my voice sounded accusing.

"I have," he said with no remorse, no shame.

No, I could see he was different than Ricky, more organized, more controlled. He probably did things that would make me cringe, but was also powerful in every sense of the word.

"Why?" I didn't know why I asked or why I even cared. But the word came out on its own, refusing to be silenced.

He didn't answer me, just watched me like a hawk about to strike.

This man could help me. This man who seemed far more powerful than anyone I'd ever come up against. I didn't know how I knew that, or why I wanted to go down this road again, but I had no other options. The words played in my head, over and over again. A cry for help was poised at the tip of my tongue. Surely a man like him, a man who could hold a gun to a stranger's head, could help me.

And you're foolish enough to ask? Isn't this how you got into your current situation?

I could see by looking into Cameron's dark, bottomless eyes that he was a man used to owning the world. And it was an ugly world. Ricky would use me up until there was nothing left.

Fucking Ricky. I should never have gone to him for help. God, poor Marshall.

Is this how David felt when he went up against Goliath? The one thing I knew for sure was that I wouldn't be getting out of this alive. Asking Cameron Ashton for help was the equivalent of asking the devil to promise not to drag me deeper into hell.

I'm already in hell. How much deeper can I get?

Neither of us said anything, and I had a feeling I could stand here all day and he'd just watch me, being the calculating bastard that I felt he was. I didn't know why he'd brought me to his office. But I assumed he'd known, or at least sensed, that I was in trouble. Or maybe he just wanted to fuck with me. He'd been watching me this whole time, that feeling of being watched more literal than I'd ever imagined.

"Why did you bring me in here?" Saying the words, questioning a man like this seemed almost abhorrent, like I was basically asking him to snuff me out.

"Why did you agree to come here?" he threw back, his voice still calm, still so damn collected.

"I need help." And the words just came out, like spilled water refusing to stay in the glass. It was a thick string of letters mashed together. I didn't want to wait for him to say anything, for him to be the one to start this, if he even would have.

Still he was silent. Still he watched me as if I intruded on his time, his space, even if he had called me here.

"I have nowhere else to go, and I assume that's why you brought me here?"

"Is that what you thought?" His question had a sharp edge to it.

I breathed out slowly, trying to appear calm, but I knew I was failing miserably at it. "I don't know what I thought, what to think."

He lifted a dark eyebrow, maybe waiting for me to continue or for me to shut the fuck up.

God, my throat was so thick. My heart raced, my hands shook, and I felt like I was on drugs, like I'd taken some speed and had no control over my body right now.

When he didn't say anything after that, I clenched my jaw, feeling light-headed, like I could pass out right now. Would he turn me down, beat me for being so brazen as to ask for help? Shit, why had he brought me here anyway? He still hadn't told me that much. Maybe seeing me squirm got him off? And if he agreed, what would he want in return?

Oh, you know.

But I could handle some rough sex, even if I had no experience with it whatsoever. I could be whoever, whatever he wanted me to be if it meant saving my life.

It wasn't until the earth opened up and hell presented itself that I realized my life wasn't disposable. I wanted to live, wanted to be a better person. I wanted that silver lining, that happily ever after. I wasn't foolish enough to think I'd ever get any of that, but I still wanted it, and I was willing to do anything to make sure I kept moving forward.

It seemed like forever that we stayed like that: him watching me, his focus calculating, intimidating.

"You think I'd be interested in doing anything for you?"

I couldn't deny that I was terrified for even asking this dangerous man for help. It was stupid, given the fact I was in this problem for this exact situation. "I hope you can." I swallowed. "I mean, you've been watching me. You had me come here, into your office—"

He made this deep sound in his throat, cutting me off, making me even tenser, more frightened.

"What makes you think I can help you, that I *would* help you?" His face remained a stoic mask, a stone statue. "Maybe I want you here, watch you, called you into my office because I want to defile you." The way he spoke, his voice, was like ice, so emotionless, so hard and unforgiving. I had no doubt he meant that.

I was on the verge of crying.

He eyed me for a long second. "You screamed of desperation, and honestly I'm a vulture wanting to feed off that."

My entire body went rigid, frozen to the core.

"Because that would be a lie, a bold-faced fucking lie."

His voice was so deep, so heavy, that I felt it weighing down on me, sucking me under like a current, making me hold on for dear life. I opened my mouth but closed it promptly. I didn't know what to say, how to answer. I felt like I'd fallen down a rabbit hole. But this was no dream. This was reality. It was my reality.

"Tell me why I should do anything for you that doesn't benefit me completely."

"I don't know," I said. It was the only thing I could come up with in that moment. This man didn't even have to say anything for me to be afraid of him.

His expression was stoic, his face a hard mask of indifference.

This was a mistake, a terrible, horrible mistake.

Although the truth was I'd known that deep down inside. The truth was I already had enough mistakes under my belt. What was one more?

"I can give you whatever you want, whatever you need."

He made this sound in the back of his throat after I spoke, and I didn't know what to make of it.

"You can give me whatever I want?" There was this hard edge to his voice as he looked at me. "And what exactly is it you think I want?" He moved his gaze up and down my body. I felt like he was undressing me right then, like he'd reached out and torn the clothes from me as if they were tissue paper. I clenched my hands into tight fists at my sides, but even that couldn't help the shaking that consumed me.

"I don't know," I said again, feeling stupid. *Show strength.* "I don't know anyone else that can handle my problem, that can get this asshole off my back." I took a step closer, but a blast of frigid air that seemed to come from Cameron stopped me. "He'll do unspeakable things to me." God, I sounded pathetic. "I can offer you...me."

Then maybe you should have been smarter. Maybe you shouldn't have gone to a motherfucker who uses people like toilet paper.

If Cameron cared, I could imagine he'd have said something like that. Hell, I'd said that to myself many times over. I hadn't told him what my problem was in detail, didn't know what this payment would entail, even if he did agree to help me. But I'd do anything. "I owe a very bad man money, even though I never spent a dime of it. I know they are following me." I ran my hands over my thighs, a nervous habit I'd always had. "I know they'll hurt me before I can do anything about it, make my life right..." *Or as right, as normal as it could be for me.* I shivered at the thought of what they could do to me.

"And you think I am the type of man that can come to an agreement with you, that I'd give a fuck what happened to you?" His voice was shrewd, his gaze glacial. "I don't think you realize the type of man you're standing in front of." There was almost this touch of amusement in his voice. Almost.

A criminal?

A drug lord?

A killer?

He's probably that and more. So much more.

"Tell me what type of man you are," I whispered, not thinking he'd actually be honest. I thought the corner of his lips quirked up, but it was gone before I could really see if it was there.

"What type of man do you think I am? What type of man would you need to help you get out of your situation?"

Could he hear my heart? It was beating painfully hard. "I think you're worse than them in a metal capacity, in the way you can outsmart anyone and anything." I took a steadying breath. "I think you're the type of man, the only type of man, who can help me." He didn't speak, but his gaze was unwavering. "And I hope you'll help me because you want that bleakness I have in me, that emptiness." That awarded me with a flicker of emotion over his face, but it was gone as soon as I saw it. "You want it because it matches yours."

He stayed silent. That was the worst of all.

"Please," I said, all but begging now, desperate. I'd already opened my mouth and asked him for help. There was no going back now. If he wouldn't help me, I'd be up shit creek without a paddle.

I'm already in that situation.

Hell, I'd rather be dead than think of what those assholes would do to me. Cameron certainly seemed far worse, far scarier, than what I was currently dealing with, and he'd only said a handful of words to me, only stared at me, maybe gauging how "worth it" I was.

He chuckled then, but it wasn't humorous, wasn't filled with amusement. It was the laugh of a depraved man...of the very devil himself, perhaps.

"I've always liked the sound of begging."

I bet he did.

I looked around his office. Aside from the television monitors behind him that showcased the entire club, and his desk and chair, there wasn't anything else in the room. It was like a coffin, a large, cold and frightening coffin. It was a place for someone to rot in the ground, away from anything and everything.

It was dark, like his soul, no doubt.

I didn't have anything of real value to offer—that was my problem, and how I'd gotten into this shit storm to begin with. But a man wanted one thing, and it was something I had, something I could give him in exchange for his help. Whether he'd accept it or not, deem it worthy of his time, was left to be determined.

Before I could say anything, Cameron started drumming his fingers on the desk, his focus trained on me, as if I was intruding on his time, despite the fact that he'd invited me here. I shifted on my feet, feeling very vulnerable in this moment. I could see his mind working, and whatever he was thinking about couldn't be good.

I took a step closer and saw something dark come into his eyes. I wasn't wearing anything sexy, but I didn't need to show off skin to get a guy's attention. The way he skimmed my body with his gaze told me all I needed to know.

Yeah, all men wanted something, one thing, but I was pretty sure I had something a man like Cameron could appreciate...nothing to lose.

"Tell me your name."

"Sofia Mikellson," I supplied, my voice wavering despite my desperate internal struggle to stay calm.

"Sofia." The way he said my name, the way it rolled off his tongue shouldn't have made me tingle, shouldn't have made my body tighten. He said it with this thick darkness in his voice that should have scared the shit out of me.

It did.

"Isn't asking for help the reason you're in this situation?"

It was like he'd read my mind, his words a hot poker right through me.

"Yes," I whispered, not bothering to lie.

Or maybe I was trying to jump out of the frying pan, the heat turned up so that I'd burn until there was nothing left.

I could be a slave to his desires, a submissive to his dominance. I could be his personal victim. If it meant that I stayed alive in the end, so be it. I could be whoever, whatever he wanted.

It seemed like an eternity before he finally moved, before he finally spoke.

He leaned forward, his forearms on the table, his expression suddenly intense. "You need my help, and the payment I want in return is your body...used in any way I see fit, for the duration of two weeks." And then he smirked. It was dark and dangerous, and shouldn't have made me feel anything other than self-loathing. "You'll be mine, Sofia. Any. Way. I. See. Fit."

I breathed in harshly. "Yes. Okay."

And so it was. I'd just sold myself to the devil.

9

I felt like a lifetime had passed since I'd spoken with Cameron, told him my troubles...asked him for help. But in reality it had only been a few days.

Hours, seconds, minutes, of me wondering what would happen, when it would take place. Would he scare Ricky, use his influence, whatever that might be, and make him leave me alone? Would he kill him?

I hadn't heard anything from him regarding it, and although Ricky hadn't bothered me, I felt someone watching. I swore a car followed me, that same dark SUV that I'd seen when I went to find Marshall. Maybe it was just my nerves, my paranoia slamming into me, claiming me, and dragging me under. But even if it was, I couldn't shake it. I couldn't push it away or bury it, no matter how much I wanted to.

You should just leave and take your chances.

Yeah, that was easier said than done. I had no money —none that I dared to use, anyway. And even if I did leave, where would I go? Who would I run to? And I had a feeling Ricky would just find me. Because I hadn't heard anything from Cameron either, I couldn't guarantee that he'd still help me. But I didn't think he forgot about the agreement.

I knew he didn't.

Sure, he wanted my body as payment, but he'd given me no time frame, hadn't even asked for details about what I was going through with Ricky. All he knew was the generic situation I'd explained.

But Cameron didn't seem like the type of man to go against what he said.

And that scares the shit out of me.

I felt my eyelids grow heavy, but I knew I wouldn't be able to fall asleep. I was exhausted, but my nerves were shot, the worry of life, of the situation I was in wearing me down so much I couldn't breathe. I was drowning, and there was no life raft, no one who would pull me out of the deep end and save my life.

I shifted, rolled over onto my back, and stared at the ceiling. The stain to the right of me was from a leak in the above apartment, the brown circle spread wide. I stared at it, tracing the edges of it with my gaze. The place was liable to cave on me at any moment, just snuff my life out as if it meant nothing.

And maybe it didn't. Maybe in the end it was just me trying to pretend I could survive.

I exhaled, not wanting my thoughts to go down that dark path.

I was Cameron's. He'd help me, get me out of the situation with Ricky, but the cost, the payment I was giving to him would be so much more. It would suck me dry, corrupt my very soul. I closed my eyes, but I knew sleep wouldn't come. My mind was moving too fast, my thoughts too consuming.

I felt myself relax further on the shitty bed I was on, the mattress probably having seen more ass, more disgust than I cared to think about.

And then I heard a soft sound come from the living room. It was a *click*, this little tick of a noise that seemed so loud, so menacing.

I sat up, reaching down beside the bed without taking my eyes off my bedroom door. It was cracked open, and the thought that maybe I should have shut it completely played through my mind. But it wouldn't have made a difference. There was no lock on my bedroom door, and if someone wanted in, they'd just have to slam their shoulder into it for the weak old-ass door to break open.

I felt the handle of the bat slide along my hand, and I curled my fingers around it. Moving slowly, trying to be silent, I lifted the bat up. I pushed the blanket off me, swung my legs over the edge of the bed, and when the mattress creaked, I grimaced. My heart seemed to still, my breathing stopped, and I stared at the door. I expected someone to come bursting in at that moment, but the silence stretched on. I wasn't a fool to think I had imagined the sound, not in this apartment building, not in the situation I was in with Ricky.

I shifted on the bed another inch, hearing that damn mattress creak again. I was frozen, my mouth tight, dry. And then the bedroom door swung open, someone kicking it in so hard it slammed against the wall, the doorknob crushing the plaster. I screamed out of instinct and fell to my knees. I had the baseball bat in my hand still, the wood feeling warm under in my hold. I scrambled to get up, because being in this submissive position wouldn't be good for me, would only make me more of a victim than I'd already be.

But someone grabbed hold of my hair and yanked me up. The bat was wrenched from my hold, and I saw scuffed-up boots in my vision. My head was cocked back, tears now in my eyes, the pain twisting me up.

"Brad, no need to scuff up the merchandise."

The man tossed me to the center of the room, and I landed hard on my hands and knees. I tried to get up, but a hand on my shoulder kept me down. I turned and stared into the eyes of a man I'd hoped to never see again.

Ricky.

"I realize I'm early in collecting payment, but I decided I'd get more bang for my buck if the payment was you." He grinned, a depraved sight, a smile that told me what he'd use me for would ruin me, would break me.

But I'll still be alive, suffering, wishing for death because my life will be nothing more than a vessel for another's pleasure.

"I need more time," I said, knowing it wouldn't make a difference, knowing the deal was for Cameron to handle this. But I grasped on to anything, something.

"Time isn't what I'm good at giving, baby." He took a step closer, and I held my breath, watching him. "And let's be honest." He cocked his head to the side. "You weren't going to repay me. You couldn't. The moment you came into my place of business you thought I'd let you off the hook." He grinned again. "You knew"—he got down on his haunches.—"the moment that money touched your fingers that your body would be used in ways you never knew possible. Deep down there was no doubt that you'd be fucked so hard the only thing you'd know for certain was that you were crying." He stood again, looked around my apartment, and tsked. "What a fucking shithole. I'll be doing you a favor."

My hands were shaking, my thoughts whirling as I tried to think of how to get out of this. I knew if I just accepted this, it would be over. I'd be over. When Ricky crouched in front of me and went to reach for my face, I curled my hand into a fist and lashed out. I slammed my knuckles into his face, and when he reeled back, I stood and darted for the door. But the guy he'd brought with him was on me before I reached the exit. He tossed me back, my head cracking back on the floor.

"You're a spunky bitch, I'll give you that," Ricky said.

I pushed myself up as best I could, the pain in my skull pounding through my entire frame.

Ricky rubbed his jaw, the grin on his face telling me he liked that I'd hit him...that he'd get me back soon enough.

"I got some guys that will pay a lot of money for you to fight them."

Chills raced up my spine.

He reached for me again, but just then the front door opened. There was no force behind it, no wood splintering forward, violence promised. No, someone who didn't need a show, who didn't need to let anyone know the menace they held, did this. I felt it as the cold air rushed into the apartment and the two men surrounding me turned.

And there stood Cameron with the man who I assumed was his muscle standing beside him.

Before anyone could move, Damien lifted his arm and fired off a shot that had the guy Ricky brought falling to the ground. The gunshot was quiet, the silencer making the violence almost seem gentle.

I couldn't move, couldn't even breathe. If Cameron hadn't shown up when he did—again—I knew I would have been hauled away and used for strange men's sexual gratification.

But him being here at the right time couldn't have been a coincidence. Had he been watching me? Had he been waiting until this moment to step up, to claim what I'd offered by ending my problem?

"How did you know?" I found myself saying, knowing I should have kept my mouth shut, but the words tumbled out of me on their own like they needed an escape, too.

He didn't show any emotion as he stared at me. He didn't answer. I was his property, so surely he'd keep an eye on me.

Either way I couldn't feel anything but this bone-searing relief, because what Ricky had planned would have made death seem like a gift.

Damien moved close to Ricky, pressed the gun to his forehead, but didn't pull the trigger. "On your knees," was all he said.

I didn't know if I expected Ricky to fight back, but it was clear he was at least smart enough—or maybe just too terrified—to know these men were not to be fucked with.

He went right to his knees.

Cameron walked over to Ricky, the air suddenly hot, the feeling of suffocating intense. Cameron gave a nod, and Damien sheathed his gun right before he started wailing on Ricky. Punch after punch landed on Ricky, his face becoming bloody, swollen, like freshly tenderized meat.

I gasped.

"That's enough, Damien" Cameron said after what seemed like hours.

Although I had no doubt Cameron could hold his own, could gift anyone with his violence, he used Damien to extract that, to be his fists, his rage.

Damien hauled up Ricky so he was on his knees again, the man wobbling, clearly having a hard time keeping upright. The sounds that came from him were gurgled, wet...blood-filled.

I glanced between Cameron and Damien—his muscle. His killer. Damien looked stoic, aloof, like he didn't give a shit what was happening. He had just beat the shit out of Ricky like this was an everyday occurrence.

You stupid girl. It is. These men are dangerous, far more dangerous than what you were up against. You'll become ruined, broken, a shell of what you were or ever could be.

And I'd signed up for this, all but begged Cameron to help me. *You agreed to do anything, everything.*

I looked at Damien's hands, his knuckles busted up, Ricky's blood covering them. His arms were crossed, his face a mask of pure violence. He was a man comfortable with death, with killing.

Just like Cameron...the man who now owned my body.

Cameron was collected, calm, but I could see the anger, the rage simmering right below the surface. He wore a suit, the dark fabric molded to his strong, hard body. The white shirt underneath the jacket had the first few buttons undone at the collar, his chest and neck tattoos a stark contrast to the light-colored material.

My heart was thundering, and I felt like I could pass out.

His dark hair was short, cropped close to his head, styled like he didn't give a fuck. And I knew he didn't, because a man like him cared only about what he could gain, what he could own. He wouldn't have gotten where he was in this life, in *hell*, by caring about anyone but himself.

Then I watched as Cameron produced his own gun, the dark violence swirling around him despite the composed aura he held. He cocked the gun, his gaze locked on me. No emotion, no fucks given as he stared at me.

"He's been hurting you," Cameron said matter-of-factly. "He hurt you right now." I couldn't move, couldn't even rise from the floor or say a word about this. I was a slave to my emotions...and I'd be a slave to Cameron once this was all said and done.

I opened my mouth, maybe to say something, anything, but the words failed me, the air thickening. I was sweating, my hair sticking to the sides of my head, beads of perspiration dotting the valley between my breasts.

"You want your trouble to go away?" Cameron asked.

I was frozen, not even able to think coherently at the moment.

"You want to be free of this pain, of this nightmare?"

Still I couldn't speak. I glanced at Ricky. He watched me, one eye swollen shut, blood covering his face. He didn't seem strong now. He knew his number had been pulled and he'd be dead before the night was over. I knew that, too. I also didn't give a shit. He deserved this. Ricky knew who and what he was up against, and he knew this was the end of the road for him.

Maybe that makes me a monster, too, because I don't care. I want him to suffer, to be afraid.

"Sofia," Cameron said my name softly, urging me in that deep, commanding voice of his.

"Yes," I whispered, my voice empty, just like my soul. I turned and faced the man who'd ridden in like the very devil himself. But then again, wasn't I the match to this gasoline-saturated scene?

"Say it. Ask me for it." Cameron's voice was eerily strong, collected.

I looked at Ricky again, a man who would have done horrible things to me, trying to push my humanity down. I should feel nothing. I should want him to hurt as much as he'd planned on hurting me, using my weakness to benefit him.

"Ask me to take your problem away." Cameron's voice was low, a little seductive. I glanced at him again, feeling like I was lost at sea.

Cameron was powerful and wanted to exert that, wanted me to be on my knees as he showed me what he could do—figuratively and literally—what he could solve. I was at his mercy, the same as Ricky. And a part of me knew that once I said the words, everything would change. Once I told Cameron what I wanted, that I wanted Ricky gone, dead, the life I knew, albeit shitty, would become something else.

I'd be the epitome of darkness, embracing it because I'd taken a life in my hands and extinguished it.

"I want my problem to go away." The words that came from me were cold, detached...just like my soul in that exact moment. I saw the way Cameron's lip lifted, this sardonic, sadistic smirk coming into play. He would have killed Ricky without my prompt, without me begging. But here, now, making me ask, that was him showing me the control he had over me.

It was the promise of what he'd show me once we were alone and I had to pay my dues.

"Say it," Cameron said again, harder this time.

I swallowed, squeezed my hands into fists, and said the words that would change the very person I thought I was. "I want him dead."

It happened in slow motion, the world rewinding, the air being sucked out of the room. Cameron lifted his hand, his hold steady on the gun, his body seeming corded, tighter. Ricky begged, pleaded. He cried and shook uncontrollably. It didn't matter, because his fate had already been sealed.

He knew what it felt like for me, how his life was now in someone else's hands. *Good.*

And then the sound of the gun going off filled me, surrounded me. It was an echoing in my head, rocking me to my core, shaking everything inside of me. Warmth seeped over me, seemed to seep *into* me.

Blood. Hot, viscous, life-sustaining fluid covered my face and chest. I was frozen in place, my body numb, the feeling of that liquid dripping from my chin, from the very ends of my hair and onto the floor, stunned as much as it disgusted and pleased me. I looked down, this humming in my ears, this vibration starting deep in my belly. I looked at Ricky, who now lay on the floor just a few feet from me, the bullet having gone right through the center of his forehead.

Just like his friend.

"Look at me, Sofia."

There was this buzzing in my head, this war drum in my chest.

"Look at me," Cameron said, harder this time, commanding me to obey.

I slowly lifted my focus from Ricky and looked at Cameron. He wore a mask of indifference. He tucked his gun at the back of his waistband, held out his hand for me to take, but I felt like I was going to throw up, like I was spinning out of control.

This is what you wanted, what you knew would happen.

I stared at his hand, feeling tears running down my face—or maybe it was Ricky's blood.

"Take my hand," he said, his voice even, nothing wavering from him. I found myself looking at Ricky and the guy he'd brought with him again, my throat closing, my body feeling like it would shut down.

And then I felt someone help me up, strong hands under my arms, lifting me as if I weighed nothing. The scent of Cameron filled me: dark, heady, and powerful. I tilted my head back and glanced at him. What did he see when he stared down at me? Did he see a broken girl who had nothing else to lose?

And when he lifted his hand, I felt myself flinch. I didn't think he'd hurt me, but after what had just happened, my body was on the defensive. I watched his jaw clench, wondering what emotion he was experiencing. Did a man like him even feel anything? Did he experience warmth, sadness, regret, or fear?

No.

No, a man like him only cared about power, about bringing fear in others.

"Damien will have the bodies disposed of."

My mind was a whirlwind, my body on autopilot as Damien led the way. We walked down the stairs of my apartment building, and I turned back and looked at my door. I knew I'd never be here again. Even after the two weeks was up, I couldn't go back. The money was still hidden, maybe forever, or maybe it would be gone, lost like I felt right now.

"The money. My things," I found myself murmuring.

"All your needs will be met." Cameron's voice was low, pitched only for my ears.

Before I knew what was happening, I was outside, the air feeling colder than it should. And there, sitting right in front of me, was that dark SUV I'd been seeing around town, following me. I would have thought it was Ricky's, but when Cameron opened the back door and ushered me in, that went right out the damn window. Once inside I stared at Cameron, not sure what to say, what to do. But before I could utter a word, he moved closer. Every part of me felt in shock, frozen to this seat.

"You've been following me," I said, my voice empty, my entire body, mind, and soul frozen.

"Yes," Cameron replied without remorse, without any shred of emotion at all.

"Why?" He'd only seen me that first time in the alley. Did he feel sorry for me, or want to hurt me as Ricky had? But as that thought played through my mind, I knew that wasn't the case. He could have done far worse than Ricky, could have denied helping me if he wanted to harm me.

He stared at me with this indifferent expression on his face. "You...intrigue me."

I intrigued him? Like some kind of pet he saw in the window and just had to take home? *That's what I am to*

*him now, his pet, his plaything. He's known about me, been
following me since before I went into his office, since before I
begged him for help.*

I didn't know what to make of that, if I should even
put any stock into it at all. Did it really matter in the
long run?

He reached out and ran his thumb across my cheek,
no doubt smudging the blood that covered me, painting
my flesh with what my life was now. "You've never looked
more beautiful to me than you do right now, with the
reality of what you've gotten yourself into smeared across
your face." His voice was deep, commanding. He moved
his thumb down to my mouth, painting my lips with the
violence that surrounded us, with the blood of the man
who would have destroyed me. "I'm going to open you up
to my world, little girl." He lowered his head so we were
now breathing the same air. "I'm going to show you what
it means to be owned by the very devil himself."

10

The car ride to wherever Cameron was taking me was done in silence. The only sounds I let penetrate were that of the vehicle moving forward and the rush of the wind that came through a crack in the window when I pushed the automatic button and rolled it down. I didn't need that rush of air, didn't need to make it seem like I was escaping either, even if I was. I wanted something to drown out the noise inside of me, the confusion and screaming that was driving me crazy.

I don't know how long we drove, but it had been hours. I was lost in my own thoughts, but I was aware of my surroundings enough to know I was going far away. Maybe that was for the best. Maybe leaving the grim horror of my world behind was what I needed. I was tired, but I couldn't fall asleep, couldn't allow that freedom to take me away, even for a little while.

It had been dark, late when we'd left my apartment, but now the sun was starting to rise, the sky being painted a pink hue, maybe promising a new beginning. But who was I kidding? I didn't have a new start anywhere. I had a future that would be laid out, set forth, planned, expected.

Cameron would control everything, and as much as I should loathe that and instinctively want to fight it, a part of me welcomed it. A side of me that didn't want to think or deal with anything, not even myself, would embrace the control I'd given him.

The car started to slow, and I turned and glanced out Cameron's window. I could see him watching me out of the corner of my eye, but I wouldn't look at him, wouldn't give him that power yet. When the vehicle came to a complete stop, I stared at the massive home in front of us. I still felt Cameron watching me, maybe appraising what I thought or how I felt. Right now I was just numb.

"Welcome home for the next two weeks."

I did look at him then, his voice deep, making me feel like I was on a wire, these flames barely licking at me from below.

The back door was opened, and a rush of wind blew in, shifting my hair over my shoulders, having the smell of blood rising up, this metallic scent that made me sick and think about what we'd left behind. Cameron got out of the car first, but I sat there, not sure what to say, how to actually move.

I was frozen in place, my mind a whirlwind, my thoughts jumbled together. Cameron leaned forward, bracing his hand on the frame of the door, his focus trained right on me.

"The sooner you come inside, the sooner you'll be acclimated to the situation."

His voice was smooth, maybe even coaxing. I wasn't a fool to think he would be gentle, that he'd give me time. I wasn't stupid enough to think he cared about my feelings whatsoever.

Of course I had no choice. I'd agreed to be his if he saved me. He'd held up his end of the deal, and now I needed to as well. In the end I reached out, slipped my hand into his, and allowed him to help me out of the SUV. I'd follow through with my end. But what frightened me most of all was the fact that fear wasn't the only thing I felt.

Arousal burned in the deepest depths of me as well.

I didn't have much time to take in the house once outside the vehicle. It was big, with giant white pillars in front, the lighting pointing to the double front doors, and the windows grand with this filigree design covering the glass. It was an elaborate, extraordinary prison, one meant to keep others out, maybe even keep some in. I noticed several men stationed close to the house, and knew there were probably more hidden in the shadows. I didn't know much about Cameron, nothing really, but I had a feeling I'd learn a lot about him in my time here.

We entered the house, and a man in a dark suit greeted Cameron. They spoke low, too low for me to hear what was being said, but I was too focused on my surroundings anyway. Dark granite, hardwood, and a crystal chandelier made up the foyer.

There was a staircase in front of us, one of those like I'd seen in *Gone with the Wind*, which started on both sides, curved upward, and branched off in opposite directions. I'd never been around so many lavish things, such taste and expanse.

I turned in a half circle, gasping slightly when I realized Damien stood right behind me. His dark eyes and aloofness set me on edge. This man was dangerous; that was clear. He might not show emotions, might not even experience them, but what he had was loyalty to Cameron.

It was that loyalty that made a man violent, willing to do anything and everything to ensure the situation went exactly how it was supposed to. That went a long way in ensuring I was kept in line, even if I had no plans on making things difficult. After two weeks I'd move on, live my life—or try to at least.

Damien stayed silent, his composure, his ramrod stance, bringing this frigid chill to my body. The tattoos I could see that crept up his neck made him seem even more imposing, even more menacing. No wonder Cameron kept him close. This man screamed danger.

"This way," Cameron said deeply, softly. I tore my gaze from Damien and followed Cameron up the stairs, the carpet beneath the hardwood making my footsteps light, silent. This home seemed to go on forever, and I found myself noticing the lack of warmth here. No, this wasn't a home. This was a place where Cameron stayed.

We continued down a long hallway, the few pictures I saw seeming dark and gloomy, depressing and frightening. Splashes of red and black, twisted birds with their beaks open, crying out. I felt like those birds, like those paintings. I was trapped, my world seeming bleak and one-dimensional.

I had no escape, not just because I was now with Cameron but because my world before him had been a dead end. I'd been trapped in my own roundabout, going around until that's all I knew.

He finally stopped at a set of polished dark wooden doors, the grain moving vertically, the gloss almost blinding. When Cameron pushed the doors open, turned on the light, and stepped aside, I didn't hesitate to walk in, to accept this with open arms.

Open arms? Who am I kidding? I'm accepting this on my hands and knees, crawling, submitting, pleading for the answer to come.

And it would come, in some form, in some way. And it

would be Cameron saying the words to me, telling me what the future held.

I pushed all thoughts out of my head. Having a clean slate, a white wall was how I would manage, how I would keep my sanity.

The room was large, the bed to my left imposing. Dark wood, fixtures, and everything in between told me this was a room that held no warmth, no life. The curtains were partially opened, but I couldn't see outside, not with the sun barely rising and the glare on the glass. I stared at my reflection, distant, blurry. It's how I felt on the inside too.

Cameron shut the door, the click resounding, as if sealing my fate, wax on an envelope. I watched him, all hard muscle bunching under his expensive suit. His tattoos peeking out from under the cuffs and collar were the only indication of the monster who lay beneath all that refinery.

"You'll sleep in here, with me." His stance screamed he wasn't about to bend to this, that he wouldn't give me an out. "The bathroom is there," he said and pointed to a partially closed door to the right. "Clothing in your size is already in the dresser and armoire. You'll shower, eat, and then sleep."

He wouldn't start this now, wouldn't break me before the sun fully rose? I saw the way he lifted his brow. Were my thoughts projected on my face? Had I said those words out loud?

"I'm not a good man, Sofia, but I won't be a bastard... not at first. Now, bathe, dress, and food will be here when you're done. I have some work to do, so you'll have to eat and sleep alone for this first time..." He moved closer to me, and I swear my heart jumped to my throat, trying to suffocate me, strangle me. "But for the next two weeks, Sofia..." He reached out and cupped my chin, tilting my head back, making me look into his dark, bottomless eyes. "For the next two weeks you'll be mine." I felt him smooth his thumb over my jawline. "When I'm done with you, walking will seem impossible."

Although I'd known he wouldn't go easy on me, I just hoped I came out of this alive, that I was still breathing in the literal sense.

11

For a moment, just a second, just a sliver of time, I didn't know where I was, didn't have any worries or cares. It was that moment right before consciousness, right before light dawned on me and I remembered my reality, when I drifted through this pleasant feeling. That second right before being fully awake.

That's how I felt that first time waking up in Cameron's bed, surrounded by his things, smelling his scent saturating the air.

I stretched, the sheet moving along my body, the silk of the nightgown I'd found in the dresser after I got out of the shower feeling smooth. Everything he'd gotten for me, every outfit, every stitch of clothing seemed intimate, handpicked by him. Although that was most likely not the case. I'm sure he'd had someone do it, paid them to pick out the silk nighties, the lace bras and panties, and the hundred other outfits that lined the drawers and shelves.

But the thought of Cameron touching these things, picking them out just for me, wanting to see me in them, tear them from my body, had every part of me on fire. There was a knock on the door before it was opened. I gathered the sheet to my chest and pushed myself up. An older woman came in, dressed in a standard maid outfit. Her graying hair was piled in a tight bun at the nape of her neck, and the clean linens she had in her hand were stark white.

She set the sheets down and turned to face me. "Do you require assistance getting ready before breakfast?"

I clenched the sheets in my hand. "Assistance?" Since arriving here I'd been so exhausted I'd slept the day away. Having people wait on me, interacting with them, the possibility of them actually knowing why I was here, was too much. "I'm fine getting ready myself."

She nodded. "Breakfast will be served downstairs. Mr. Ashton is already waiting for you." She then left me alone, and I relaxed. This was all so weird on its own, but to realize there was staff here, knowing, hearing what would go down, had this awkward feeling consuming me.

I glanced at the spot beside me and ran my hand over the perfectly placed sheet and comforter. It was cold to the touch, letting me know Cameron hadn't been in here all night. That confused but also pleased me, like this weight had been lifted from me, even though a part of me wanted that heaviness.

I waited until the maid left before I got out of bed and got cleaned up in the bathroom. Once I was dressed, staring down at myself, rubbing the lace material of the dress between my fingers, I finally took a deep breath. This was the first day of the rest of my life, right? Or at least my life for the next fourteen days.

I opened the bedroom door and just stood there for a second, listening, watching. The upper floor was quiet, the dark walls and equally ominous decor making things appear cold.

The sooner you do this, the sooner you'll see how things go. The quicker this will be done.

Steeling myself, trying to grab on to my courage, I stepped into the hallway and closed the door behind me. My palms were sweating, my mouth dry. I forced myself to walk, made myself do this, be strong. I'd made this agreement, and I needed to see it through. When I saw that black bird painting, his eyes so dark, yet seeming to stare right into my soul, this chill raced up my spine.

I don't know how long I stood there, the dark colors mixing together, his beak open, his cry silent, yet I could hear it in my head. I turned and made my way down the stairs, assuming I even knew where the dining room was where I was to meet up with Cameron. Everything was so still, so...lifeless.

When I finally found the dining room, the wide

double doors were engraved with this detail around the edges, maybe trying to soften it, make it appear gentle. It failed, or maybe that was because the man who owned this place, resided within these walls, was cold like ice and unbreakable like granite.

He didn't look at me as I entered, but then again I hadn't assumed he would. I'd only been in his presence such a short time, but he was the type of man that moved at his own pace. He didn't stop what he was doing for anyone.

A side door opened, and I got a glimpse of the kitchen. Several servants came in, silver platters in their hands, their focus trained on anything but the man at the head of the table. I took a second to look around, looking at the floor-to-ceiling windows that lined one whole wall, the dark accented decor, and the frigidness I felt surrounding me. I was still standing there when the servants left.

"Sit, Sofia," Cameron said, still looking down at the paper in front of him.

I made my way toward the seat across from him. The table was long, easily seating sixteen. Yet I still felt as though we were seated intimately, like he was right beside me. The plate in front of me was white and empty. I reached out, seeing my hand shaking, feeling the nerves in me rise. I had my fingers wrapped around the crystal, the orange juice in it almost trembling from my shaking hand.

"There's nothing to be nervous about."

I glanced up, startled, surprised to find that Cameron was staring right at me. He grabbed his cup and took a long drink, watching me over the rim. When he set the cup down and leaned back, I felt on display despite my body being covered.

"You slept well?"

I nodded. "You didn't sleep with me." I meant it in the most basic of senses, him beside me, the mattress dipping from his powerful weight. But I suppose it could be taken literally and figuratively.

"That was the only night I won't be in bed with you."

I had no doubt about that.

"Eat up, because you'll need your energy."

It was hard to be hungry, to have any kind of appetite when my stomach was in knots. The question I wanted to ask him was on the tip of my tongue, yet I didn't know what the ground rules were, didn't know what he did or didn't want me to know.

And I won't know until I ask him.

But I kept my mouth shut. I grabbed some fruit and a piece of buttered toast and started eating, keeping my mind and mouth occupied so I didn't cross that line. Silence stretched between us, but I embraced it.

"If you have things on your mind, it's best we get that done now."

The bread was dry in my mouth, and when I went to swallow, it lodged in my throat. I coughed, grabbed my water, and took a long drink. Cameron was staring at me, watching me the same way a hawk probably did the mouse before it snatched it up and devoured it.

"What exactly do you plan on doing with me?" Sex was the obvious, but what I meant, what was on my mind, twisting me up, was how far Cameron wanted to go, how far he'd push me. Would he break me? Did he want to ruin me?

"You're worried I'll hurt you." Cameron didn't state it like a question. "You're worried what you've agreed to is a fate far worse than what you were in." Again it wasn't a question.

I looked down, not responding, because he already knew that was what I wondered, what I feared. I couldn't deny my attraction to him, couldn't lie to myself and say he didn't make me feel this rush of awareness.

He was a dangerous man who'd killed someone for me, because I'd asked. He could do whatever he wanted to me and I'd have no choice but to accept it, not just because I'd agreed, but also because a small part of me craved it. This twisted part of me wanted whatever he had to offer.

The pain and pleasure, the coldness yet warmth he gave me with just a look. This man was a monster, and I was more than willing to let him destroy me.

What was wrong with me? What kind of person did that make me?

When I heard his chair scraping, I glanced up.

Cameron stood, set his napkin down on the table, and came closer. I was frozen in place, unable to breathe, to even think. On instinct I rose, maybe to appear bigger, stronger. It didn't help, though, not when the only thing I could hear was the thundering of my heart in my ears and the feeling of my belly doing flips.

And then he was right in front of me.

He was so close, his body, his presence so consuming. For long seconds he didn't speak, didn't even move. He reached out and touched a lock of my hair, toying with the strands between his fingers, focused solely on it.

"All I want, what I desire, is your surrender." His voice was pitched low I knew if anyone else had been in the room they wouldn't have heard him. "I'm not a good man." He said it so matter-of-factly that I had no doubts whatsoever that this man knew who and what he was. "I'm a killer, a drug lord." He took another step closer. "I rule the underground with apathy and violence." His chest was so wide, so powerful that it took up my entire view.

"I know who and what you are." But did I really?

He shook his head slowly. "No, I don't think you do, Sofia. I don't think you do at all."

I was sucking air into my lungs, hard, fast, yet I couldn't breathe.

"I feel you're my weakness," he said softly, his voice deep, like a knife skating along my body, barely touching me, but the threat of getting cut was right there at the surface. He lifted his head then, staring me in the eyes, his gaze so cold, so hard. I was small, miniature compared to him. "And having a weakness isn't something I'm comfortable with."

I shivered after he spoke, not because of the chill in the air and not because of his dark, deep voice. I did it because of the way he was looking at me. I didn't need to know Cameron personally to understand a man like him didn't do weakness. He was all strength, all power.

Before I knew what was happening, he leaned forward, reached around me, and pushed the plates and silverware to the side. The china clinked together, the glass spilling water along the white tablecloth. And then he had his hands on my waist, lifting me onto the hard, unforgiving top.

I reached behind me, bracing my hands on the linen, half of it wet under my palms. The heat from his body penetrated me, made me drunk, intoxicated with everything that was happening. Two weeks was short in the grand scheme of things, so the fact he wasn't waiting to take me wasn't all that surprising.

"Spread your legs," he said, low, demanding that I do what he wanted.

The rational, survival part of me wanted to ask him what he had planned, what he'd do to me. But the smart part of me said, *Shut the fuck up and do what he says.*

I stared into his eyes and felt him smooth his hands over my inner thighs, pushing up the bottom part of the dress I wore. It was light, summery, and the feel of the material sliding over my skin had goose bumps popping out over my flesh.

When he was a few inches from the most intimate part of me, he exerted pressure and spread my thighs even wider. I swallowed, my throat feeling tight, dry. He moved his hands an inch closer, and I felt myself start to respond, felt my body heat come alive. I should have feared him, maybe even been disgusted, repulsed by what he probably wanted to do to me.

But I was wet.

"How affected are you right now?" he asked, his sweet-smelling breath moving along my lips. He moved his fingers even closer. I knew he had to be touching the edge of my lace panties now. He leaned in until there was only an inch separating our mouths. "Answer me."

I licked my lips, searching his face, trying to read him. It was no use. This man was unmovable, unreadable. "Affected" was all I said, all I knew how to say in this moment. Actually saying I was wet, that I was ready for him, that this form of control and torture—albeit arousing me to no end—made me so on edge I would give it to him without a fight.

I saw something dark flicker in his eyes, but he didn't show emotion any other way.

"If I touch your cunt, would you be wet?"

I didn't make him wait for an answer. I nodded.

"If I stroked your little clit, would you come for me?"

Again I nodded. I knew I would, knew it wouldn't take me more than a few hard, fast strokes of his finger on my clit to bring me off. He lowered his eyes to my chest, and I knew he was watching the way my breasts rose and fell, fast, almost violently. The white shirt he wore was unbuttoned at the collar, and the tattoos I could see looked angry, harsh…untouchable.

They matched the man in front of me.

I shifted, maybe to move away, to get some air. Maybe I was suffocating from my own desires, the need to be with this man so intense my fear and pleasure slammed together. They fought, my common sense telling me this wasn't what I should want, that my body reacting this way wasn't normal.

"Are you frightened of me or of this situation?" He smoothed his finger over the edge of my panties. "Does it scare the fuck out of you, what I plan on doing, that the unknown is right there, teasing you, tormenting you?"

I didn't know if being honest was the right course, if admitting that yeah, I was afraid but I was also turned on, would actually be the wisest decision.

"You're terrified right now, but I can also tell you want this." He leaned in another inch, our mouths so close. "Your cheeks are pink, your pupils dilated." He lowered his gaze to my mouth. "You're breathing so hard right now, your breasts pushing against the material of the dress." He lifted his gaze back to my eyes. "I bet you feel like you're drowning."

I felt myself pull my legs apart even more, as if my body had a mind of its own, was controlling this situation...was seeking out more of Cameron's touch.

He made this deep, dark sound, this noise of approval, this tone that told me he liked what I'd just done.

"You want me to taste you, to lick you until you come?"

I shivered, my flesh tightening, my pulse racing.

"You want me to run my tongue through your cunt, suck at your clit, and show you how good I can make you feel?"

I didn't know what to say, didn't know if he actually wanted me to answer. And then he placed his hand right between my thighs, right over my wet pussy.

"Tell me what you want me to do, beg me for it."

He got off on me saying these things, on the humiliation I felt succumbing to my desires, submitting to him. I felt a flush steal over me, my entire body on fire, my skin sensitive to the slightest breeze in the air. He added even more pressure, making me gasp, my toes curling.

"Fucking tell me what you want, and if you're a good girl, I might give it to you."

"I want you to touch me, to lick me," I whispered.

He made this low growl, this animalistic sound. I could hear people in the kitchen, the bang of pots, the clatter of china. They could come through that door right now and see me on the table, my legs spread, with Cameron's hand between my thighs.

"What else do you want?" He added even more pressure, and I closed my eyes, a moan ripping from me.

"I want you to make me yours." God, I'd just said that out loud, told him exactly what he wanted to hear, played into his hand.

"Good girl," he all but purred, his mouth by my ear, his hand still between my legs. "Your honesty deserves a reward." And then he was on his haunches between my legs, his warm breath moving along my panty-covered pussy.

He didn't make me wait long to wonder what he'd do, how far he'd go. He pulled my panties aside, the dual combination of his warm breath and the chilled air sending shock waves through me. I wanted to scream, beg, plead for him to touch me, to lick me, to ease the raging arousal burning deeply in me. He either read my mind, or maybe I said the words out loud. Or maybe he just couldn't stand it any longer either.

Before I could even think about what was going on, before I could grasp the reality of my situation, I felt him move his tongue through my folds, parting me, making me shiver. I wanted more, yet I wanted to push him away, tell him I didn't want this...convince myself of this fact.

He continued to lick at me, dragging his tongue through my lips, circling my clit, sucking the bud into his mouth on every upstroke. I grabbed the tablecloth, held it tightly, my nails digging through it and spearing my palms. A gasp left me when Cameron gently bit my clit, making this high-pitched cry leave me and having me gasp for air. I yanked on the cloth as pleasure and pain consumed me.

The sound of something clattering to the ground and shattering vaguely pierced my mind. I was trying so hard not to enjoy this, to fight myself on what he was doing to me, how he made me feel so free, so alive. His hands on my inner thighs were rough, painful. He held me in place as he opened me up to his tongue and mouth, to his beautiful torment. It was pleasure and pain all wrapped into one conflicting ball, into one war inside of me that wouldn't surrender.

And then he thrust his tongue into my body, my pussy clamping on the muscle, dragging it farther in, needing it as deep as it would go. I wanted to be stretched, claimed completely, and in this moment nothing else mattered...my body, my situation, my very reasoning for not wanting this man.

None of that mattered right here and now as the pleasure washed through me, dug its nails into my body, hanging on, not letting go.

I felt the tendrils of that delicious, depraved pleasure wash through me. I should have fought it, rebelled against it, but instead I found myself welcoming it, embracing it. And just as I felt the pleasure crest, Cameron pulled away.

I sagged against the table, my body shaking, the near orgasm leaving me breathless and on the verge of wanting to beg him to make me feel good, to wash away the bleakness in my life.

"Open your eyes."

I found myself obeying him instantly. He still had his hands on my inner thighs, but he was no longer between my legs. His focus was trained on me, his lips red from what he'd just been doing to me.

"You stopped." I didn't know why I thought it was a good idea to say anything, but the words came from me fast, breathless. He didn't speak, didn't even show emotion. He'd just been eating me out, yet his expression showed me nothing. He was like a brick wall, a poker face that would crush all others. I shifted on the table, trying to close my legs, but Cameron still had his hands on me, holding me open, making me feel vulnerable.

The door to the kitchen opened, and in walked one of his waitstaff. My heart thundered, embarrassment filling me. But Cameron seemed unaffected, not taking his hands from my legs, not breaking eye contact.

"I'm the one who holds the power, Sofia." He moved a step away, running his big, tattooed hands on his pants as he stared at me. "You'll be whole once this is all said and done, and I'll let you go back to the life you know...if that's what you want."

If that's what I want?

"But you'll do best to remember that I'm the one you

owe, that I'm the one who pulled you from the recesses of hell. For the next two weeks you're mine." He looked me right in the eyes. "Finish eating if you want, then get cleaned up and meet me in the solarium." And then he turned and left, leaving me on the table, my legs spread, and the waitstaff on the floor picking up the shards of broken glass.

I felt like that china on the floor: cracked, vulnerable, at the mercy of another. And I knew this was only the beginning.

12

I had to ask someone where the solarium was, and once I stepped through the glass doors, the heat and scent of sweetness filled my head. There were trees, plants, even a waterfall that cascaded into a small pool off to the side. There were no walls, not even a ceiling. It was all glass, and the sun streaming in made the room hot and slightly humid.

I didn't see Cameron, so, assuming he wasn't here yet, I took some time to explore. I'd never seen a solarium before, didn't even really know what one was. This over-size greenhouse was incredible, magical even.

The smell of the many varieties of flowers filled my head, making me slightly drunk from the purity of it. The sound of the water crashing onto the rocks of the small pond almost had a lulling effect to it, calming me.

Through the windows I could see a vast expanse of

trees, thick pines and evergreens, ones that blocked out anything and everyone. I had a feeling it was something Cameron preferred. His privacy seemed pretty paramount. Just thinking about him had my body warming, my erogenous zones tingling. He'd brought me to the brink of coming; then like a sadist he'd backed off, leaving me cold and hungry. When I'd been straightening up in the bathroom, before I'd come down, I'd thought of touching myself, easing my arousal so I could get a little bit of relief. I'd refrained, though, from teasing myself any more. For some reason I wanted Cameron to be the one to finally break the dam in me, the passion and pleasure he'd brought right to the surface.

I found myself walking toward a row of beautiful white flowers. They were almost wispy and dreamlike, soft and innocent. I ran my finger over one of the petals, the softness what I had expected. I was transfixed as I watched my finger move along the flower, over and over, smoothing, whispering along it. And then I felt the hairs on my arms stand on end, that feeling of being watched consuming me.

When I glanced around, I didn't see anyone at first, but the feeling that I wasn't alone was too strong to ignore. I was about to turn back to the flowers, maybe move to another part, try and shake the feeling, when my gaze landed on a darkened corner.

Then I saw him watching me, the shadows concealing him, making me feel very aware that we were the only two in the room. On instinct I glanced at the doors, seeing they were now shut. When I shifted back to look at Cameron, I felt his gaze on me, this intense feeling like a second skin going over me, covering me.

"Come here," he said, his voice clear despite the high glass ceiling and the waterfall just on the other side of him. I felt myself move toward him, as if my body knew the routine, knew the path I had to take.

I was only a few feet from him when he held his hand out to stop me.

"I gave you a treat after breakfast." He leaned forward, his face coming into the sunlight, his expression severe... aroused. "But this is about *me*, about *you* pleasuring me in any way I see fit." I felt like he would have smirked at me then, but he kept his cold composure. "Isn't that right, Sofia?"

The way he said my name did all sorts of filthy, wrong things to me. I found myself nodding. Yes, that was true, so true I felt it in my very bones.

"Now, undress for me."

I could do nothing but stand there for a second. Having him see me nude wasn't a shock. No, it was the way he'd demanded it, his voice like ice: cold, hard, able to hurt without trying. I was here, alive, for one purpose, and that was to please this man, to bend to his will, and give him whatever he wanted.

It was true when I said I'd be his victim...his willing, already wet victim.

But what I hadn't factored in was the fact I might actually enjoy this...want it.

Anyone and everyone could see us, and a part of me grew even more aroused by that, even more on edge. What was wrong with me? Why was I enjoying this, finding myself wanting it?

I pushed all thoughts out of my head. They wouldn't do me any good, wouldn't save me. *Is that even what I want?*

Once I was undressed, my motions unceremonious, I stepped away from my clothes scattered on the floor around me. I felt my heart jackhammering agasint my ribs, like the muscle wanted out, needed to escape the depravity that was about to happen. But despite my fear, the knowledge that Cameron had more darkness in him than the very night, I anticipated this.

I wanted this.

Even now I was wet, ready for him, needing him inside of me, taking from me the way the entire world had for my entire life.

He hadn't told me to remove my clothing slowly, to make a show for him. I had a feeling a man like Cameron wasn't about teasing. He wanted the reward when it was due.

I noticed the small table beside him, the glass filled with what I assumed was alcohol. I guess it wasn't too early for mind fucks or getting drunk.

Cameron lifted his glass, the liquid within the cut

crystal seeming darker than normal. He brought the cup to his mouth and took a long drink from it while watching me over the rim. The room seemed so cold with him in it, yet here I was, sweating, beads of perspiration rolling down my nude body, chilling in the air. The sun was a constant presence around me, the purity and beauty of our surroundings about to be tarnished and broken by what he wanted me to do for him.

He had his shirtsleeves rolled up, his thickly corded forearms, inked in abstract designs, frightening displays of power, flashing before me like a promise. His hands were so large, and I could imagine them holding me down, pinning me beneath him as he took me, claimed what he was after. After a second he set his cup down and just watched me, as if he enjoyed seeing me on edge, seeing me fragile...at his mercy.

"Get on your knees," he ordered, demanding my submission, my compliance.

I found myself falling to my knees, the tiled floor unforgiving, reminding me where I was, who I was here with. I stared at Cameron, his body partially obstructed in the shadows.

"Come to me, Sofia."

I wasn't fooled by the low pitch of Cameron's voice. He was like a snake: hypnotic, seductive, but striking when I least expected it. And so I came to him, crawled to him, my body shivering, my mind racing. I wasn't cold, wasn't even frightened in this exact moment.

I shivered, breathed in hard, and tried to focus because I was turned on.

I wanted this, wanted him to show me the black hole that was his soul, that had been my life. I knew he could give me that. I knew he'd want to give it to me as much as he wanted to take from me.

When I was in front of him, my knees aching, my palms sweating, he did nothing but look at me for long seconds. But I sat there, waiting, holding my breath, knowing he'd take me when he was ready. He'd bend me to his will when he deemed it so. His body was big, corded with muscle. The tattoos that lined his neck and chest could be seen through the crisp whiteness of his shirt, past the open collar of the persona he showed the world.

"Look at me."

I lifted my head, my gaze to his face. He leaned forward, dusk slashing across the harsh beauty of his face, showing me what lurked beneath the surface of this monstrously gorgeous man.

"Ask me for it. Beg me for it."

My throat tightened, my mouth grew wetter, and every part of me was tense. It was like an electrical current washed through me, lighting me up, bringing me to life.

"Ask me for it," he demanded and instantly gripped my chin, his hold unforgiving, brutal even. I'd have bruises on my face, my skin matted with the blue imprint of his passion. And to Cameron this was his passion, roaring out at me, demanding that I give in.

And a part of me wanted that, needed that mark of his ownership marring me, showing me that this was real, that I was truly alive.

"Please," I finally whispered. I felt him tighten his hold on me, knew that one word, that submissive word, struck him deep.

"Again."

I licked my lips, seeing that he stared at them. He looked into my eyes now.

"Again, Sofia, and say my name this time." His words were like a whip to my flesh, opening me up, making me bleed.

"Please...Cameron."

His groan was the most emotion I'd ever seen from him, the biggest reaction he'd ever given me. For long seconds he just stared at me, holding my chin in that painful yet surprisingly erotic grip. He smoothed his thumb over my bottom lip, pulling the flesh down before letting it fall back in place. As the seconds moved by, the minutes, I was transfixed by the sight of him, by his touch. And then he let me go, and I felt as though I were falling into the abyss. He leaned back and undid his belt before undoing his button and pulling the zipper down on his slacks. I felt like I couldn't breathe, although I knew I was, sensed my chest rising and falling violently.

When he pulled himself free, his cock thick, long,

hard for me, I did stop breathing then. I didn't move, didn't even contemplate taking control and starting this. Cameron was the one who held the reins, who would begin this when he was ready.

"How much do you want this?" he asked and gripped himself, not stroking his length, just holding it. I stared into his eyes, wanting to lie, to say I didn't want it, but the truth was the opposite.

I did want it. I wanted the pain and pleasure I knew he could give me, not just from his power and strength controlling me, but because he knew what I was about. He really knew.

"I want it."

He leaned forward an inch, and I smelled the alcohol he'd been drinking. No doubt it had been expensive, maybe even burned when it slid down the throat. It made me feel drunk, intoxicated with wanting more. "Tell me," he demanded, his voice fiercer now.

"I want it like I want to take my next breath." Maybe a little overboard, but it was right on point with how I felt at the moment.

The low sound he made had me growing wetter. I clenched my thighs together, wanting pressure, wanting his hand there, touching me, bringing out the filthiest part of my desires.

"Do you like the fact I own you? Do you like the knowledge that you agreed to be mine in every way I see fit, any way I see fit?"

I nodded, because right now my mouth wasn't working, my lips not forming the words.

"Yeah, I bet you do." He had his hand on the back of my head, gripping my hair, yanking me backward so my throat was exposed, arched. The pain was intense, and tears pricked my eyes. But it also felt so good, so freeing. "If you want it, take it." He tightened his hold on my hair even more. "But make it good, make me pleased to have you here, that it was worth it bringing you out of hell."

Out of hell? Wasn't I in it, basking in the heat of the flames, the touch of the devil himself?

He pulled my head forward until the slick tip of his dick moved along my lips. His hold on me was unforgiving, a promise that he did hold the power, that he'd control the situation.

"Open up and suck me until I tell you to stop." He yanked my head back again and looked in my eyes. "And don't stop until I tell you to, Sofia. Understand?"

I nodded.

His words and actions shouldn't have made me so aroused. Was I so broken that his rough touch could incite these emotions in me, could make me crave him like an addict for their next fix? Or maybe I wasn't broken at all. Maybe Cameron and I were exactly the same, sharing the same bottomless soul that had dragged me down but raised him up. Maybe what made me feel alone made him feel alive.

He pulled me forward again, and I opened, taking his

girth and length into my mouth. The flavor of Cameron was heady but also elusive, like the man himself. He didn't make a sound for me, so I didn't know if what I did pleased him. The only reaction he gave was a tightening in my hair and the tenseness of his thighs under my palms.

I closed my eyes and got lost in pleasing him... needing to make him feel good, to see that he and I weren't so different. He could make me feel something more with just a look, just a touch to my cheek. I wanted to make him feel that way, too, wanted to show him that I too could have power.

So when I focused on pleasing him, I did it with everything in me. I swirled my tongue around the crown of his shaft, tasting the saltiness of his male essence. I clenched my legs impossibly tighter together, the feeling of my wetness coating my inner thighs, a telltale sign of how much I wanted him making shame and excitement wage war in me.

I got lost in everything Cameron. I flattened my tongue, running it up and down his length. Still he was quiet; still he showed me no reaction. It made me frenzied to have him unravel the way he made me unravel.

The longer he was in my mouth, the more control I felt I had. I took hold of the root of his dick and stroked what I couldn't reach with my mouth. He still had his hand in my hair, keeping me stationary, a slave to my actions.

But then something shifted...he shifted. He gently lifted his hips, pushing another inch of himself into my mouth. I took as much as I could, moaning around him, unable to hold in the sound, not wanting to. The tip of his cock hit the back of my throat with every thrust of his hips. I gagged, tears stinging my eyes, rolling down my cheeks.

"Look at me," he said, his voice husky, as if I were affecting him and my reward was this slight crack in his armor. With my gaze locked with his and his hips doing the work now, thrusting in and retreating between my lips, I could do nothing but hold on as he found his pleasure.

The tears continued to stream down my face every time he lodged the tip of his shaft at the back of my throat. I felt high, like any moment now I'd reach the very heavens.

Cameron cupped one side of my cheek, and I saw the way his jaw clenched, knew he was on the precipice of coming, of surrendering to *me*. I breathed in and out through my nose, not trying to stop this, not trying to push him back. I wanted to taste him, to have his cum in my mouth, sliding down my throat. I wanted him to force me to take it all.

And then he buried all his hard, hot inches into me and came. And I swallowed every last drop.

His hold on my hair was brutal, the pain very real, but it was coupled with the desire I had for him, the fact it was because of me that he'd let go. He pulled my head back, his semi-hard shaft slipping from my mouth. I felt a little of his cum slip out of the corner of my mouth, and as he looked at me, I swiped my tongue over it. I wanted every last drop of him in me.

When he let go of my hair, only then did I sag forward, my hands on the floor, my head lowered. I closed my eyes and sucked in much needed air, my lungs burning, my mind and body on fire. I felt his finger under my chin, lifting my head up so I had to look at him again.

He leaned down and ran his tongue over one side of my face, licking the wetness away. "The sweetest flavor on my tongue is your tears." He pulled back slightly, his face so close, his warm breath brushing along my cheek. "And you'll give me more of them, so much more before our time is done, Sofia."

13

I could have gotten lost in a home this big, with so many rooms it was an endless labyrinth. The cold floors were unforgiving on my bare feet, and although I could have put shoes on, blocking out the rigid feeling, putting a barrier between the two, I liked the sensations. It made me feel like I was here, that I wasn't dreaming, wasn't conjuring up this entire situation.

After the solarium encounter Cameron had gotten a phone call. He'd excused himself like we hadn't just done something dark and...good? God, I didn't know anymore, didn't know what to think, didn't know if I should embrace what I felt and ignore the nagging in the back of my head that told me I shouldn't want this. But the truth was I did want this. I was tired of the feeling of being nowhere, yet surrounded by everything. I didn't fit in anywhere, and I realized that in Cameron's presence. I might cry for him, my body instinctively wanting to submit, but being in his presence told me exactly how fragile I was.

It made me realize I really was here, experiencing the world.

But I'd never been one to freely give in, never been a woman who just took what the world gave her. I'd fought for where I was, even if that place was shitty and broken down.

I stopped in front of the window that overlooked the gardens. Despite the April weather being somewhat warm, I saw the wind pick up, brushing along the leaves, telling me that it was colder than it looked. Putting my hand on the glass proved my point, the chilled pane bringing a sting to my palm.

The house felt still, empty, and the only staff I'd seen were those few during breakfast, when I'd first arrived, and the woman who'd come into the room just this morning. I had a feeling if Cameron had been there she wouldn't have dared enter. He just brought out the instinctual fear in people. That much I'd felt myself.

I moved my hand from the glass and turned, making my way down another long hallway, and stopped at one of the only open doors I'd seen so far. It looked like a sitting room, or what I assumed one of those rooms would look like if I'd ever been in one. Dark furniture was placed in the center, and large windows were on either side of the room. The marble fireplace sat unused, clean, pristine, as if it was just for show. Behind me were rows upon rows of books, and although I wasn't much of a reader, I did find myself moving toward them. Old leather-bound books which spoke of age, time, stared back at me. I ran my hands over them, the ridges on the spines a texture that pleased me for some reason.

No pictures. Nothing personal.

The thought came to me like a flickering light on its last leg. Why weren't there any pictures of Cameron? Why did this seem so impersonal, this entire home— house—as if he didn't really live here? So many questions filtered through my head, yet I knew I'd probably never have the nerve to ask, let alone get them answered.

I pulled one of the books out, the writing on the front in another language. There was a vine and flower detail around the edge of the front cover, an embossed signature, the book's fingerprint. As I started flipping through the pages, unable to actually read the book, unable to understand the language, I felt myself getting engrossed in it. It was beautiful, the letters placed perfectly together, the detail in each chapter...it was all so detailed. It was like a dream, an imagination that couldn't be erased.

I closed the book and gently slid it back in place among the others. When I turned, a startled gasp left me. Cameron stood in the doorway, his hands in his front pockets, his gaze locked on me. Neither of us moved, didn't even speak for long seconds.

"You've been exploring." He didn't phrase it like a question nor an accusation.

I smoothed my hands over my dress and nodded. My body hummed with awareness, his close proximity, the things he'd done to me...made me do to him ringing through my very cells. "Yes," I finally said. It was then I saw the dark security camera placed in the center of the room. No doubt there was one in every room, every hall-way. "You've been watching me?"

He didn't speak for long seconds, didn't answer me, didn't confirm what I asked. "Yes. I watch everything that happens here." He pushed away from the door frame, holding his hand out for me to take.

For some reason I didn't hesitate in slipping mine in his much bigger palm.

He led us out of the room, back through the many hallways, down a set of stairs, and finally into what I assumed was his office. I didn't ask what he was doing, why he'd brought me here. I assumed it had something to do with sex. That's why I was here, right?

He let go of my hand, went over to his desk, and pushed a button. Like some strange spy movie, some action flick that played out before me, a part of the wall behind his desk opened up to show rows upon rows of screens. Every part of the house was showcased before me, the screen flickering to different areas, inside and outside, bedrooms and the kitchen. I found myself moving closer, looking at the screens, seeing a few staff in the kitchen cleaning up from breakfast. I didn't know how long I stood there, but I watched each screen, staring at each image, and wondering what Cameron thought about when he saw me.

I felt his heat right behind me, his huge body making me feel like I could fall backward and he'd be there, catching me, holding me close. It was insane, demented, but I didn't want to push that feeling away. I wanted to embrace it.

He put his hands on my shoulders, slid them down my arms, and stopped at my hips. His fingers dug into my flesh, hard enough I felt the pain, the sting of his possession. And when Cameron pulled me back against him, the stiff length of his erection had this flush stealing over me.

"I've watched you on these screens, wondering what you thought about, what you imagined would happen here." He ground himself against me, my body reacting instantly. I warmed, became wet, soft. "I thought about all the things I could do to you, what I wanted you to do to me, how I wanted you to submit to me like no other."

I closed my eyes, the rotating of his hips, the way he whispered the words against my ears...all of it made me ready for him, had me pushing away the fact I shouldn't be enjoying it.

"Who are you?" I whispered, not sure why I asked, not sure what this meant or what he'd think. He stopped grinding on me, turned me around gently, and cupped my throat. His hold was loose but there, telling me, showing me that he had the power.

"Who do you think I am?" He didn't ask it in a condescending manner, wasn't taunting me, teasing me. I had a feeling he really wanted to know what I thought.

I stared into his dark eyes, remembering all the things he'd told me about himself.

Drug lord.

Criminal.

Killer.

I wanted to know who he was. I wanted to know the type of man he was before he became this way. But asking him that seemed almost like I'd be crossing a line, something I wasn't prepared to do, not yet, maybe not ever. But the longer he stared at me, looking into my eyes, the more I felt myself wanting to ask, wanting to push him. I might not have gone to school in the official sense, didn't have a degree, couldn't read people the way he could, but I could see a man with so much power also harbored his own pain.

"I think you're a man who has seen things he shouldn't, a boy who is just as damaged, just as broken." I felt him tighten his hand on my throat, just marginally, but his expression still stayed neutral. "I think you built up a wall around you, put yourself ahead of everyone, because you didn't have any other choice." I was grasping for straws here, just throwing this out, thinking a man like Cameron had to have his own weaknesses and that's why he needed so much power. "I think you need to have control, because once in your life you had none." He walked me backward until I felt the wall of monitors stop me. "I think that's why you don't have anything personal here, no pictures, no memories. You have a wall around your life to block it all out." His hand was tight, unforgiving on my throat. I couldn't breathe, but he was exerting his strength on me.

For long moments he did nothing but hold my throat, keeping me pinned to the wall, staring into my eyes. And when he leaned in close, his mouth inches from mine now, I held my breath, unable to control it.

"Careful, pretty girl. You're moving awfully close to the fire, and if you're not careful, you'll get burned alive."

That, I had no doubt about, but a part of me wanted to get swept up in the flames, consumed by them. I wanted to be the gasoline that ignited it all.

14

I t had only been days since I'd been here. Well, it had only felt like days, but maybe it had been longer, time meshing together, coming as one.

I was curled up on a bench, the sun setting, the husky pink glow of dusk washing through the window. The book I was reading was one of poetry, sad, longing phrases of love lost, of pain, sorrow. I stared out the window, thinking about the author, how they must have been in a dark place to write these words, to spill them along the pages in dark ink of emotion.

After the encounter in Cameron's office, he'd left me to "settle myself," whatever that meant. But I was thankful for this time alone, my thoughts my company, the scenery my comfort.

I set the book down and got up. I wanted to go outside, to get some fresh air. I didn't care if it was chilly, and if I didn't have a jacket. I was also shoeless, but I anticipated the feeling of that chill on my soles, and the texture from the ground seeping into me.

After I left the room, I headed down the hall and to the solarium. I hadn't explored the lower level much, so wasn't sure where the actual back entrance was. But it didn't matter in the end, because I'd make it outside regardless. I didn't see anyone on my way to the solarium and was curious if Cameron would let me explore outside alone. It wasn't until I pushed open the large glass door that led to the gardens that I stopped when I saw Damien standing just a few short feet away.

No, it seemed Cameron wouldn't let me roam alone.

I clenched my teeth, that fact more than annoying. I was here of my own free will and had no intentions of leaving. He'd just find me anyway.

"I don't need a chaperone. I'm not going anywhere. A deal is a deal." I had no idea why I even said anything to Damien. The man hadn't said anything to me and always had this look of indifference and danger surrounding him. I didn't expect him to respond, and when I started walking away, feeling him following at a distance, I figured at least if I had to have someone with me, Damien was as good as it would get. He'd keep his mouth shut and at least make it seem like he wasn't really there.

After some time I pushed the fact he was behind me out of my head and enjoyed the scenery. There wasn't much in the growing department as it was early April.

But some of the more common bulbs had already begun sprouting, the promise of color and life in the air. I hadn't come outside to look at what wasn't here. I wasn't to be outside to be free, to not have any walls surrounding me, to have the fresh air and sun on my skin. A breeze moved by, chilled, the hint of winter's past in its touch. I shivered slightly and wrapped my arms around my waist. When I sat on a stone bench, the seat cold, hard, unforgiving, I stared at the woods that surrounded the property. It went on for as far as the eye could see, a natural fence, a blockage of green and brown.

In the corner of my eye I saw Damien off to the side, his huge arms hanging loosely at his side, his focus on me. I turned and looked at him, wondering where this man had come from, who he was. How long had he known Cameron? Did they share the same fucked-up past? I might not know what that past was, but the reaction I'd gotten from Cameron when I brought it up told me he had his own demons he dealt with.

"I'm really not going anywhere. You can tell him that." I felt like saying the words, pushing them in further, making him see that I was here because I wanted to be.

Because I wanted to be...

That thought played through my head over and over again, and I realized that although my circumstances were pretty fucked up, being here wasn't the worst thing in the world. Although I might not have seen the full extent of what Cameron wanted to do to me, so far he hadn't hurt me, hadn't made me feel degraded. He'd fed me, provided clothing—even if it did feel wrong at times. It was all so confusing, but I realized I was welcoming it, in some regard at least.

I don't know how long I sat there in silence, but then again I didn't expect him to respond, didn't expect him to grace me with anything. I pushed my hair off my shoulder, the wind like a lost lover's caress, gentle, cold.

"I'm not here because he thinks you'll leave."

I turned and faced Damien, startled that he'd said something.

"I'm here to make sure you're safe." He glanced at me, his dark eyes cold, his expression neutral. I didn't ask what he meant by that, didn't ask why he'd decided to tell me. Cameron was a dangerous man, I knew that, and I had to assume it was because of that, because he had connections, that he was looking out for me in that regard...because I was his property.

Was he saying I wasn't safe from Cameron's enemies, or maybe he was being truthful, telling me that who I should really be afraid of, who I was really in danger from was Cameron.

"But if you have any fear, you shouldn't. This property is secure." He did glance at me then. "I'm just the extra measure." He broke eye contact and stared off into the distance. He'd said more words to me than he ever had before.

I, too, looked out at the trees, not sure what to think,

how to feel. Maybe I should have put more stock into what I wanted, into the fact that my desire played more of a role in this than my fear. Maybe I should have been worried, but instead I felt like I embraced it, like I wasn't even giving myself a chance to not accept this. I glanced at Damien again and took in the several guns I saw strapped to his body.

"Should I be afraid of him?" I whispered, not sure if Damien would even answer, not sure if I wanted him to. He slowly turned his head in my direction. But before he said anything, if he even planned on saying anything, I felt as if someone was here, watching us.

"Sofia," Cameron said from the doorway, his voice deep, mesmerizing. I turned to stare at him.

My heart was already stuttering in my chest. He looked fierce in this moment, maybe even angry with me for pushing him earlier. Had he heard what I'd asked Damien?

"Go to the bedroom. Undress, and wait for me." The fact he didn't mince his words in front of Damien had my face heating, embarrassment swimming through me. And then he was gone, leaving me there with my mind reeling. Tonight I'd find out exactly what he had in store for me. The oral he'd given me, and when I'd done it to him, had just been the appetizer to this twisted story. I knew that, felt it.

15

I found myself in the bedroom, taking my clothes off as if it was an automatic gesture. I thought about how I'd felt outside, the wind in my hair, the sensation that nothing contained me, nothing held me back, a familiar feeling since I'd been with Cameron. I was in the process of pushing my panties down when the bedroom door opened. I turned, my heart thundering, my mind spinning. Cameron shut the door behind him, the suit he had on not taking away from the sheer presence that surrounded him.

"Damien is there for protection, not conversation," he said as he started to remove his tie, his focus on me.

I swallowed, not sure if I should hold my ground or back away. I couldn't help but feel like he was stalking me, moving forward slowly, waiting for his chance to attack. There wasn't anything I could say, nothing I wanted to say in that moment. He kept moving forward, tossing the tie on the bed. Then he went for his cuff links. It was then, once he had them off and set on the vanity, that I realized I was stuck between him and the wall. There didn't seem to be any way to stop this.

Do I want to stop this?

Yes, I wanted to scream out. *I want this to stop.* I shouldn't have to compromise myself because my body warmed at the thought and sight of him. This man made me feel things that I wanted to keep buried, hidden. I felt like my own body was working against me, succumbing, submitting to this man...this monster.

This is insane. *You are insane.*

I couldn't help thinking that over and over again, disgusted with myself and this man, because not only did I fear him, but I wanted him, too. A gorgeous demon intent on corrupting me, determined to make me his.

"You can ask anyone about me." He moved a step closer. "But if you want the truth, you'll ask me directly."

I was a prisoner of my own body, my mind. "Asking you anything directly seemed like crossing a line." He was just inches from me now, his body so big, his heat so intense. Before I could contemplate what he was going to do, what he might say, he had his hands on my waist, turning me, and setting me on the vanity.

The apothecary jars crashed to the side before rolling off and shattering on the ground. Here I was, ready for him, my mind screaming to preserve my self-respect, to let him know that I was strong.

"Who are you really?" I found myself asking, my voice breathy, my body ready. He had his hands on my waist still, holding me, caressing me. I wasn't a fool to think this man would be gentle, not in the parts that counted, not when there was fucking instead of making love.

No, Cameron was definitely the hate-fuck kind of guy, the one who took what he wanted because he knew he could. But then again, I wasn't a flowers-and-chocolate girl. I'd come from the gutter of the world, fought my way to the surface just so I could breathe, and the darkness Cameron offered was what I craved.

"Who are you, Sofia?" He slid his hands up to my bra straps, slid them over my shoulders, but didn't remove the garment. "Tell me you don't want what I can give you, that you aren't wet with the idea of the depravity in which I can cover you completely." He smoothed his hands over the mounds of my breasts, which rose violently above my bra line. "Tell me that taking you in the way I want to, crave to, doesn't make you so fucking ready for me you're on the verge of begging me for my cock."

His words should have shocked me, had bile rising in my throat. Instead I found myself moaning, unable to control myself, unable to control the most basic urges I had for him.

"So tell me, sweet Sofia. Who are *you*?"

We stared into each other's eyes for a long second, my

mind a whirlwind, my throat tight. "I'm the girl who sold herself to the very devil himself, right?"

He smirked, the first time I'd seen anything but hard composure on this man's face.

"Who are you?" I asked again, not sure if this was smart, not sure if just playing out this time wasn't the best route for me to take. After that I could go, live my life, be away from it all. I'd find a way to leave, to forget about what I'd gotten myself into, what I'd seen. The death, the violence, the fear I felt when I didn't think I had any options with Ricky—those things didn't have to control me. They didn't have to follow me for the rest of my life.

He slid his hand up to my throat, added a bit of pressure, and leaned in. "I'm a man with a past you don't want to know about."

But I did want to know about him. I did want to know how he became the way he was, this powerful person who was deadly, intelligent, and mine for the next two weeks.

That last thought slammed into me so hard I made this involuntary sound, this breathless gasp.

"Tell me what you just thought about right now," he said, moving an inch closer, my legs spread, his erection tenting the front of his slacks and coming into contact with my pussy. He felt so hard, so big. I was a virgin, never even been with a man before. This would have scared me with a "normal" man. Cameron was anything but normal. He was dangerous, probably volatile, and the things he wanted to do to me...I shivered at the images.

I contemplated about lying, about making something up, or maybe being submissive, subservient. I thought about just telling him I made the sound because I was eager for this, or maybe scared of it—the latter being the truth. He added a bit of pressure to my throat, and I braced my hands on the vanity, rising up slightly. I arched my neck, wanting the pressure off, wanting him to add more.

He held me like he had a right to, like I wanted this, would beg him for it eventually.

I'd probably do that now.

What I was fighting myself on was the fact that these things he said to me, did to me, humiliating as they were, turned me on.

"I thought about how I'm yours for the next two weeks, but that you're also mine." Being honest seemed like the best course, but truthfully I probably wouldn't have been able to force the lie out anyway.

He pulled back and stared at me, barely breathing, not moving.

A part of me didn't want to desire him, didn't want this. But I couldn't fight it. I didn't want to.

"You want to know the man I am, Sofia?" The way he said it, the look in his eyes and the deepness of his voice, startled me. He was like an animal waiting to pounce on his prey, just take the weaker creature and devour it.

And I was that weaker animal.

He moved back from me, his hand leaving my throat. He started undoing the buttons of his shirt, pushing the material off his shoulders, and I was left speechless as I stared at the body before me. I'd been able to see how strong and muscular he was even when he wore a suit. Thick biceps, vein-roped arms, a defined six-pack and that V that framed it, and tattoos covering it all.

It wasn't the ink that startled me, but the thick scars I saw underneath. Ones that looked like knife wounds, maybe even cigarettes burns? There was an array of other nasty-looking ones that could be made out if I looked hard enough. The ink did a good job of camouflaging it all, but they were there, a testament of the violent life he'd led. Were they self-inflicted or brought on by another? Had he been held down and tortured, or freely accepted his fate? The words slammed into my head, the questions replaying over and over again.

"The monster I am is on the inside and outside, Sofia." He moved toward me again. My legs were still spread, and he stepped between them, his body heat seeping into me. "I never pretended to be someone I'm not." He tilted his head to the side, his focus on my mouth, his dark eyes like coal. "Beaten as a child, sold into an illegal underage fighting circuit, I made sure I stayed alive. That's all I knew how to do." He had his hands on my thighs, his fingers long, rough. He added a little bit of pressure. I knew he could snap my bones with ease, his strength not something he showed. It was just who and what he was. "Love and affection is not something I know, not something I will ever embrace." He slid his hands up my thighs, over my belly, along the curve of my breasts, and wrapped them around my throat once more.

There was no fear in me, despite my heart thundering and my palms sweating. The feeling of his hands on my neck was comforting, secure.

"The love I learned was fists slamming into my body, blood filling my mouth. Eating, breathing...surviving, meant I fought my way to the top." He moved an inch closer, his hard cock pressed to my pussy again. "That's the type of man I am, the only comfort I know." His mouth was so close to mine, his warm, sweet breath moving along my lips. "But I saw you, and this obsession grew, this possessive need to have you, claim you as mine." He looked me right in the eye, maybe willing me to understand the severity, depravity of what he meant. "And for the first time in my life I wanted something soft and sweet."

Could he hear my heart beating, see how rapid my breathing was?

"So you know who I am, see what I am." He moved his hands down my arms, squeezed my wrists, then moved them behind my back. "Keep them there." He then lowered himself to his haunches, placed his hands on my thighs, and wrenched them open until pain sliced through my muscles.

I was wrapped up in a delusion that I was his, or maybe it wasn't delusional at all. Maybe I was his, in every way, and in the end I'd be this twisted, warped, desperate person, needing his touch, aching for it.

"So pink. So wet." He looked up at me, the shadows playing across his face. He leaned forward, and I held my breath. "Make noise for me, pretty girl. Scream, lash out if you want. Pain and pleasure make one strong emotion that's undeniable."

I squeezed my eyes shut. I shouldn't want to feel good, but God, I did.

And when he ran his tongue up my slit, swirling along my clit, the noise did spill from me then.

"Never deny me, sweet girl," he said against my soaked flesh. He ran his tongue up and down my pussy, lapping up my arousal. "Never deny me and I'll give you the fucking world on its knees, bowing to you." He gave my pussy one last lick, causing me to shiver. He rose up, moved his thumb along the pulse right below my ear, and said, "Always be my good girl and you'll reign over it all."

I didn't know what that meant, didn't know if I wanted to know.

He had his hands on my waist, and in a second he had me flipped over, my belly on the vanity, my ass popped out. God, he was so strong. Cameron had my hands still clasped behind my back with the slightest discomfort.

Everything happened so fast. My heart spun. My pulse raced.

The feeling of his warm breath on my ass had me glancing over, seeing him kneeling behind me. He pulled my ass cheeks apart and stared at what he revealed. I was dizzy, my world rocking on its axis, twisting, turning. Uncontrollable.

"You smell so sweet, so innocent, and mine." He squeezed my flesh, a sharp sensation that claimed me, grabbed hold and wouldn't let go. "You're so fucking wet for me, for the fact I want to defile you, do things to you that you've never imagined." He growled low in his throat, this animal feral, stalking.

He moved his lips over the top of my ass and took hold of each of my cheeks in his big hands. He just held his hands there, not doing much but kissing my flesh, running his teeth along the mounds.

"I know you hate this, that you fucking loathe the fact you're greedy for me, your body primed, ready for my invasion."

The cry that left me was more from arousal than anything else. He smoothed his hands over my waist, gently, almost caringly. But then he dug his fingers into me, making me still, holding me in place.

"Oh *God*." I tried to move away from his erotically abusive mouth, knowing that I shouldn't want this. It was this instinct in me, this fight mode that had my toes rising, my heart thundering.

"You already crave me, my touch, my mouth on you. And my cock will soon be filling you, stretching you." He ran his teeth along my flesh, and a violent shiver worked its way through me. "My need for you, my obsession knows no bounds."

"This is twisted, insane."

"Sweet girl." He was tormenting me with the promise of forced ecstasy. "Trying to fight me makes this better, turns me on more." He groaned deeply. "I want all of you, your emotions, the sensations you feel," he said and placed a finger by my pussy opening. "I want your words, the screams of your orgasm, the pleas for me to stop." He pulled the digit away, never fully penetrating me, just staying right there at the cusp. "And when you beg me to stop, cry out for more, I'll make you see that there is no end." And then he did penetrate me, but not where I thought he would.

He moved his tongue along the secret part of me, the spot hidden until he'd displayed it, pulled my ass apart. His entire focus was there, making me squirm, making me hate myself for wanting it so much. I was lost in the sensations, in the feeling of him running that muscle up and down me, teasing the hole, gently prodding it. He made me take it, made me want it.

With his hand on the center of my back now, keeping me there, making me accept this, I felt the air leave my lungs. I didn't know if someone could get off from this, but the intense sensations I felt made me realize that anything Cameron did to me, I'd want ten times over.

Tears tracked down my cheeks, my emotions so turbulent I couldn't control them, didn't want to. The hand still holding on to my ass gave a hard, painful squeeze. Cameron licked that dark, secret place once more, then pulled away, spun me around, and stared me in the eyes. I was still crying, unable to stop.

"Maybe I don't want this." The sweet, salty flavor of my tears slid down my cheeks, a path of sorrow, of need. I didn't know why I said anything, why I felt the need to kick the hornet's nest. I cried because the emotions, the sensations were too much, too intense. He placed his hand right between my thighs, right where I ached for him. I opened my mouth on a silent gasp when he started rubbing my clit. The pleasure built inside of me. Cameron made this deep, humming sound.

"Lies. Fucking lies, Sofia." His hand holding my waist was bruising me, no doubt having purple and blue marks forming on my pale flesh. "With me you'll only tell the truth. And if I have to force it out of you, make you come as you say the words, so fucking be it."

I knew I couldn't lie. My body betrayed the truth, denying what I said. I tried to stay strong, distant. And then he wrenched the pleasure from me, reaching in deep to my very soul, pulling it out and ripping it free. I was helpless to stop myself, but truth was I didn't want to fight it, didn't want to pretend I didn't want this. I started crying, the pleasure too much, the realization of it all too much for me to take in.

"My sweet Sofia." Before I knew what was happening, Cameron had me in his arms, cradling me to his hard, powerful body, and holding me. He said things low, far too quietly for me to hear, but I didn't need to know what he said.

The atmosphere had changed, and in that moment I was here because I wanted to be. I wanted the beautiful torment he delivered, gave me freely.

I didn't push him away, didn't try to run. Instead I let Cameron carry me to the bed, knowing I was done fighting, even if it was only myself the war had been with.

16

I could see this wild look in Cameron's eyes as he stared down at me, as he looked me over like I was this feast and he was eating for the last time. There was this part of me, this loud, raging part, that wanted to submit in all the ways that counted.

Do it. Accept it. Be his.

"Spread for me." His voice was low, demon-like in its intensity, in the quality. While he stared at the valley between my thighs, he started undressing. He went for his belt, the button of his slacks. He pushed the material off, stood before me like this tattooed, scarred god that was intent on destruction.

I must not have been fast enough, because he growled low, grabbed my inner thighs, and wrenched my legs open.

"When I say spread for me, that means open fucking

wide, Sofia. I want to see what I'll be taking as mine." He dug his fingers into my skin. "I want to see your virgin cunt, all open for me like a flower, wet, needy for my cock." He kept his hands on me, his fingers in my flesh. I wanted his mark, those bruises that told me I was his property and he owned me.

My muscles strained from the force with which he held them apart. All he did was stare at me, look right at my pussy, appraise it, memorizing every line, every part that was primed.

"A virgin who likes her pussy lips bare…" He trailed off, one of his eyebrows lifting as if this intrigued him. Cameron moved his hands up my thighs until he framed my pussy, his big, tattooed fingers on either side of the most intimate part of me. "I'm going to tear you up, pretty girl."

Maybe his words should have frightened me, disgusted me, or made me want to lash out. But all I did was get wetter. He made this low sound in the back of his throat, and I had no doubt he saw the product of my desire for him coating my pussy lips.

"And you want that too." He said that almost to himself. He pulled my lips apart, and the chilled air moved along my inner folds, teasing me, making me shiver with desire. I was transfixed by him, frozen in place by the dark desire reflected at me. And then my heart stalled when he moved back, reached down for his belt, and wrapped half of it around his hand.

Maybe he saw the fear in my eyes, the worry clouding me, because his chuckle was low and deep, taunting me. "Your fear only turns me on more." I was about to push myself up, not sure why, not sure if I'd try and stop what was surely about to happen next, but Cameron stopped me. He brought the leather down on the bed beside me, making me still, having my heart stop. "Turn around; present your ass to me."

"What are you going to do?" The words were low, stuttering out of me, broken and chipped.

His laugh was deep, twisted, sadistic. I knew it was obvious, but I wanted him to say it, wanted that brutality in his words to be a reality. "Oh, Sofia, I'm going to bring this belt down on your pretty peach flesh, making it red, seeing the welts of my desire on your body." He took a step closer, the glint from his belt buckle catching the dim light. "Now, turn over and let me see your pretty ass."

The look he gave me said I wasn't to disobey. *And I don't want to.* I moved onto my belly, looking over my shoulder, needing to see this, watch this act. He wasted no time. He moved all the way toward the end of the bed, lifted his arm up, and before I could brace myself, he was bringing the leather right across my ass. I had no time to react, to process any of this because he kept hitting me, bringing that wickedly good leather down on my flesh, sensitizing it, making it burn, tingle. Hot tears of pleasure fell from my eyes, burning their way down my cheeks like Cameron was doing with that belt on my flesh.

All the while he stared right into my eyes, his look hot, pleasure-filled. He got off on this, hearing my gasps of pain, my swift inhalations of pleasure. He was getting excited by the fact he caused me this agony while gracing me with ecstasy.

"Spread even wider," he ordered, and I obeyed. I had my teeth gritted so tightly I felt like they'd break. Beads of sweat started to line my skin, a visual of how strained I was, how excited he made me feel. I anticipated this, was curious about how far he'd go. Would he be gentle this first time with me? The rational part of me screamed no.

And when he brought the belt down on my ass once more, the leather stinging, maybe even breaking the skin, I cried out.

"That's it," he said low, almost too softly for me to hear. He slipped his hand between my legs, and a startled sound left me. "So wet. You cry, but you like this."

And then I heard the clank of what I assumed was the belt hitting the floor. The weight of him covered my back, the hard length of his dick settling right between my folds. I was breathing so hard, the air leaving me, making the sheets humid, hot. I was hyperventilating. Could you pass out while lying down?

"Calm yourself," he said right by my ear.

The thick, long length between his thighs, nestled right at my pussy, was intimidating.

God. I thought for a second about how he wouldn't fit, how the pain would be too much. He'd split me in two, make me hurt, bleed in ways that had nothing to do with taking my hymen. But even though I had those thoughts, I knew he'd fit, knew he'd stretch me, make me take all of him. He'd make me feel good.

Cameron started rubbing the thick crest of his cock up and down my slit, showing me what was to come, what he offered. And when he rubbed it over my clit, eliciting a little moan from me, I felt like I'd suffocate from the pressure of it all.

"There's no going back. Ready or not, Sofia, I'm about to devour you." He pressed the head of his dick right at my entrance. My entire body tensed on its own, and I was unable to control it. His hold on my hips hurt so good. Then he pushed into me, making me take it, making me bite my lips until blood welled under my teeth and coated my tongue. The metallic flavor filled my mouth, a shock to my senses.

He placed both hands beside my head as he continued to make me take his dick. Sweat bloomed between my shoulder blades, and, as if it was a temptation for Cameron, he lowered his head and ran his tongue along the valley between them.

He pulled out slowly and pushed back. Over and over, tormenting me, making me weep with how much more I wanted. I clutched at the sheets, drawing them close to my face, saturating them with my tears, my honesty. There was darkness and light, literally and figuratively. In that moment I was his, the same as he was mine. That discomfort and pain slowly started to diminish. My virginity was gone, my virtue, innocence, in the hands of this man.

And then he started thrusting into me like the rope tethering him to reality had snapped. He slammed into me so forcefully my body was shoved up the bed. He gripped my waist, keeping me in place, making me the vessel for his pleasure...for my pleasure. The pain took my breath away, the ecstasy confusing the hell out of me. I was full, so damn full of his cock I couldn't think straight, couldn't even contemplate what was happening.

I watched him over my shoulder, saw that he was focused on where we were connected, where he impaled me. His frantic thrusting slowed, and in its place was this lazy, prolonged swing of his hips against me, pushing his dick farther into me, making me take all of him.

"You want more, want me to give you so much more you can't even breathe?" He never stopped moving in and out of me.

I felt the darkest parts of me rise, wage war with what I *should* want, *should* feel. He slid his hand up my back, moved it around to my throat, and circled my neck. The pressure, the slight feeling of him cutting off my airflow was just enough that I felt dizzy, just enough that I only felt *him*.

He was a monster, a sadistic beast. He was the only person who could make me feel like this, who could free me.

"I want more, so much more from you." He uttered those words low, sharp, like a blade over my skin. He applied more pressure to my neck, released it, and clenched around my throat again.

Dizzy, clear, twisted, alive.

I felt conflicting emotions. Cameron was thrusting in and out of me ferociously now, his skin slapping against mine, forcing his way into me, out of me. Repeat.

He plowed in and out of me, a mortar and a pestle.

"Give yourself to me, tell me that you're mine, that you want this, want all that comes with it." He pounded into me, thrusting those long, thick inches into my willing body, making me take it all.

I closed my eyes, opened myself up, and allowed myself to just absorb the sensations. I came for Cameron, feeling him stretching me beyond belief, taking me to a place I'd never even known existed. The darkness kissed my flesh, stroked its icy cold hands on my body, and held me down. Cameron pressed his hand in the center of my back, thrusting, his motions hard, powerful.

"Tell me you're mine," Cameron said in this almost violent voice.

"I'm yours," I cried out, the words spilling from me as if they were their own entity, wanting out, wanting to be free, as well. I was aware of Cameron slamming his cock in and out of me, but my mind was adrift, my body detached. I could only feel.

He made this low, dangerous sound, and I felt him get thicker in me.

"You're fucking mine," he said; then I felt him come, felt him fill me up, bathe me in his seed. He held me down, made me take it all, accept what he had to give me. The pleasure, Cameron's desire, lasted a lifetime. And when he gave one last grunt, one final thrust, he rested his chest on my back. We were sweaty, our breathing rough, hard, and I felt my body start to shake. It was like I was coming down from this incredible high, feeling this chill seep into my very marrow.

I hadn't fought, hadn't tried to survive. I'd given in to Cameron, became his willing victim, and God, it felt...freeing.

17

I stared at myself in the bathroom mirror, feeling out of place, distant. Cameron had only told me a couple of hours ago that he had an event to go to, one where I would go with him. I'd be his arm candy, and even though he hadn't said that, I'd read between the lines. I really doubted this "event" would have the legal, law-abiding type of citizens. I was afraid, even if I knew Cameron wouldn't let anyone hurt me.

I slid my hand down my stomach, over the silky material of the dress he'd given me to wear. My time was almost up with Cameron, the two weeks going in this blur of emotions and feelings. I only had a couple of days left here, and although I should be glad, my life free, I couldn't help this emptiness that filled me.

This hadn't just been about keeping a deal. Cameron

had taken my virginity, slept beside me, keeping me close. I wasn't stupid enough to think he cared for me, but did so because I was his property. But that didn't mean I hadn't grown attached to him, needing him, wanting him.

I placed my hand right between my thighs, still sore, still remembering the way he felt in me that first night. He touched me, stroked me with his mouth and tongue, caressed every part of me. But I knew he wouldn't keep that up, knew he had a limited time with me, only the two weeks we'd agreed to.

The sound of someone knocking on my door had me leaving the bathroom. Just as I walked out, I saw the bedroom door opening. Damien stood on the other side, his focus on me, his gaze cold, hard. "Cameron's downstairs waiting for you."

I nodded. He turned and left, leaving the door open. I glanced down at myself again, the cream dress form-fitting, the silk showing off my curves—what little I had, anyway. Taking a deep breath was meant to try and calm me, but it didn't. I'd noticed that being here had my body, my mind all in disarray. I wasn't nervous or afraid of what might happen. I felt this way because the excitement of being with Cameron, others' gazes on us, seeing him touch me if he wanted, simply because he could, made me anticipate it all.

Steeling myself, I straightened my shoulders and headed out of the room and down the stairs. Cameron stood by the door, his focus on his phone, his fingers moving over the keys. He was messaging someone, and I couldn't help but feel this twinge of amusement that a man such as Cameron, big and strong, scary and dangerous, was texting.

I placed a hand on the banister, curling my fingers around it, the wood cold, smooth. I took that first step, descending, my heart in my throat. I moved toward him, and he glanced up while placing his phone in his pocket. His gaze roamed over my body, and I couldn't help but appreciate the view as well. He wore a dark tux, the white shirt under it stark, crisp. His tattoos could still be seen, creeping up his throat like icy fingers of dread—or power. Cameron held his hand out to me, the ink covering the back of it frightening as well as intimidating in appearance.

When I slipped my hand in his, he curled his fingers around mine, pulling me closer, his hard body coming in contact with my soft one. He said nothing to me, just cupped the back of my hair. One of the servants had done my hair, a chignon that looked haphazard but elegant, whimsical even. And when I thought the air would leave my lungs, suffocation my last experience, he leaned down and kissed me. It wasn't sweet, wasn't soft. He took control, plunging his tongue into my mouth, claiming me, making me know he was the one who held the power.

And strangely enough, I was okay with that. Without me giving my consent about it, without allowing myself to be here, experiencing it, Cameron had no power over me. I had strength in this "relationship" too, maybe even more than he did. That knowledge, that realization was heady.

He broke the kiss but kept his hand on my neck. "Tonight is informal, more or less. You'll be free to wander, but I'd prefer you stay close. Some of the guests at this event are...questionable in their endeavors." And without another word, without waiting for me to say anything in response, he opened the door and we stepped outside. There was a stretch limo waiting, the back door already opened, Damien clearly waiting for us.

Once in the back, the door shut, the scent of leather and Cameron filling my head, I sank back against the seat to try and calm myself. The privacy divider was down, but as soon as Damien climbed into the driver's seat, he rolled it up, blocking Cameron and me from everything else. The car started moving, and the silence stretched between us. I stared out the tinted window, the sun already having set, so it was much too dark for me to really see anything. But looking out the window seemed better, safer, than trying not to glance at Cameron.

"Look at me," he said in a deep, baritone voice.

I turned and stared at him, glancing into his dark eyes, wondering what he thought about, what he saw when he stared into my eyes. Did he see a broken girl, or did he see the changes in me, the ones I felt transforming me inside since being with him, experiencing his delicious capture?

"Come closer," he demanded softly. There was a dim light in the back of the limo, giving way to this dreamlike atmosphere, this almost hazy experience. I shifted on the seat, the leather and my dress causing my movements to be water-like. Before I knew what was happening, Cameron had me on his lap, his hands on my waist, his lips on mine. I was startled, gasping, the sudden movement making me feel off balance. Cameron moved his mouth slowly yet thoroughly against mine at the same time he slipped the dress up my legs. He moved his hand over my ass, the barely there thong I wore hardly a barrier. Cameron started rubbing ever so slowly the crease where my ass met my thighs. I was uncomfortable, because Damien was right on the other side of that thin protective shield. If he wanted to speak with Cameron, he'd only have to push it down and he'd see the act we were doing.

But in the same breath that act turned me on like no other.

He slipped his hand farther down, right over my panty covered pussy. And then he moved the material aside and ran his finger through my slit, eliciting a soft moan from me. I was still sore from what he'd done to me, from how he'd stretched m, despite it being two weeks since I arrived. Even my thighs objected to being spread, straddling his muscular frame. And when he applied pressure to my clit, I gasped, knowing I could come like this.

"Seeing you like this, unhinged, at my mercy, does more to turn me on than anything else." He rubbed my clit harder, a little faster. I'd come for him soon, and I didn't want to fight it. I was so wet, maybe embarrassingly so.

The sound of his finger moving over my soaked flesh filled the back of the limo. Could Damien hear what was going on? Did he know what was happening even if he couldn't?

I opened my mouth, the pleasure building, the silent cry right on the tip of my tongue.

"Let go," he said, those two words more of a demand than anything else. And when he slipped a finger into me, all the while still rubbing the little bud, I finally let go. It was like a dam opening up inside of me, breaking free, washing through my entire body and claiming me. I gasped and found myself biting down on his shoulder, knowing it had to hurt. He hissed, but a groan still followed. The ecstasy was body absorbing, taking me further away, higher up.

And when the high faded, my body relaxed, my mind calmed, I rested against Cameron's chest. He wrapped his arms around me, the act gentle, caring even. It was so against the man he portrayed, the one who killed without remorse because he could, because he had to in order to survive.

I don't know how long we stayed like that, but Cameron held me the whole way, moving his hand up and down my back, letting me relax, be calm before the storm.

I could have stayed like this forever.

18

"We're here," Damien said through an intercom placed close to us. I lifted my head, surprised that the time had gone by so fast. Cameron helped me off him, and I adjusted my dress, making sure I was righted. Through the window I could see the massive house we'd pulled in front of. There were cars lined up, each one waiting their turn. I watched one of the cars farther up, this sleek red sports car. One of the staff opened the door, and a gorgeous blonde in an equally gorgeous ruby-colored gown stepped out. The man who accompanied her was older, maybe even double her age. They walked up the massive steps that led to the front door, and then we were moving forward.

I was still wet between my thighs, the arousal and orgasm Cameron had brought forth in me not dimming in the slightest. Blood rushed through my veins, this excitement and fear coursing through me. Once it was our turn, the back door was opened. Cameron stepped out, then promptly held his hand out for me.

I slipped mine into his much larger palm, allowing him to pull me out gently, and together we ascended the steps. My mind was whirling, my pulse racing. I could hear music coming from the inside. I wanted to ask what this event was about, but I knew better. And truth was I didn't want to know. I didn't want to know about the men who were here, ones who were most likely dangerous, just as much as Cameron.

We headed inside, and my breath was stalled in my lungs at the sight before me. Crystal chandeliers, a smoke-filled atmosphere smelling of sweetness, and servants walking around with silver trays and champagne flutes filled with bubbling liquid took up my view. I saw a few other servants with trays filled with hors d'oeuvres, the staff's backs stiff and their expressions blank.

The guests were in expensive outfits, diamonds and gems dripping from them. The men looked severe and intense as they spoke to each other. The women appeared to be more ornamental than anything else, their heads downcast, their expressions void.

I didn't miss the fact that some of the men eyed me, their gazes lewd. I felt Cameron wrap his arm around me, pulling me closer to him. I sank against his hard body, feeling like nothing could touch me. I knew he didn't have to bring me here, didn't have to show me off. He wanted to because he knew he could protect me, keep me safe. Twisted reasoning or not, I trusted him.

For the next twenty minutes we walked around. I held a champagne flute in my hand, the liquid warming in the glass because I wasn't drinking it fast enough. Cameron spoke with a few men, his voice even, the respect they had for him clear.

And then one man started speaking in another language, his voice clipped, his words clearly angry, even though I didn't know what he said. The man had gray, thinning hair, and his eyes were these thin little black beads. He stopped in front of us, a young, voluptuous, and busty woman hanging on his arm. She too had her head downcast and couldn't be more than twenty-five.

Cameron's arm was still wrapped around me tightly, but his fingers digging into my waist told me he was focused on the man he was speaking with, not realizing what he was doing. I slipped out of his hold, and he stopped speaking and looked at me.

The man started rambling off in that other language, and Cameron turned and barked out a string of words. The other man paled, his back going straight, his eyes narrowing. Cameron looked at me again.

"I'm just going to walk around, see the art."

Cameron looked me in the eyes, his gaze penetrating, intense. He finally nodded, but I wasn't foolish enough to think he wouldn't know where I was.

I walked down one of the hallways, the guests thinning as they congregated with each other at the front of the house. The art was colorful, erratic even. I kept moving, looking at each piece. There was a set of open double doors to my right, and I moved closer. I didn't want to be nosy, but the lights were on, and I saw even more art. Surely if no one was allowed in here, the doors would be shut.

I stepped inside, the lights dimmer than I'd originally thought, the corners hidden with shadows, making the art seem ominous. I walked around, the scent of old leather, roses, and something darker filling the air.

The sound of wood creaking behind me had me looking over my shoulder. A man stepped inside, his focus on his cell, his face cast in a scowl. He said something low, too low for me to understand.

He shoved his cell in his pocket, went to turn around, but then spotted me. For a second he just stared at me, his dark eyes seeming like endless pools. It gave me the chills, made me frightened. I didn't know why, but I didn't want to be in the same room with him.

"You like the art?" His voice was thickly accented.

I nodded, not sure why I felt so nervous, so off kilter. I wanted to go back to Cameron. I went closer to the door, but he shifted, blocking me.

His smile was so dark it actually made me uncomfortable. Warning bells started going off, red flags flashing in front of my eyes. I needed to get to people, to the crowd.

There I'd feel safe, just like at the club, being swallowed whole by the sea of bodies.

"Are you here alone?"

I shook my head, my throat far too tight to manage any words. *Force them out. Show strength.* "I'm not alone." The need to run, to lash out, to fight ran strong within me. I was pressed to the wall, my hands flat on it, the sweat starting to form on my palms. He moved closer, the cloying, suffocating sensation of his cologne making me sick.

I tried to look around his shoulder, but he'd backed me into a corner, the people at this event farther away than I would have liked. I was blocked by his grossly large muscles.

He breathed out hard, the scent of his liquor-laced breath wafting over me, the need to gag strong. My stomach was twisted, turned around. I was in flight or fight, my mind screaming to be rational, that I couldn't stop this man if I wanted to. But my body wanted to lash out, to survive.

"So small, fragile." He looked into my eyes, his smile grotesque. "I'll have fun breaking you, girl."

I didn't know what came over me, but this surge of power, of strength took hold, making me feel—realize—I was not this asshole's victim. I brought my knee up, rammed it right between his thighs, and felt really damn good when he made this pained sound.

"You fucking cunt," he gritted out. He was slightly

hunched, and I knew he wanted to grab himself, relieve the pain I'd caused, but instead he raised his hand. I knew he'd hit back, knew he wouldn't stand for me attacking him. I wanted to move, tried to in that instant, but his big body blocked me.

I tensed, bracing for the hit, but before it came I saw a shadow cross over his body. Then a hand grabbed his arm, pulling back with a force that had him stumbling.

The big brute cursed in Russian. Although I didn't see, couldn't see who held him away from me at this angle, I knew it was Cameron.

I felt it in the air, this charge, this intensity that stole my breath, made me weak, had me shaking. And then the Russian was jerked back and I saw Cameron. He looked furious, enraged, his eyes cold, dead.

I shifted, seeing the man's face now, the fear that covered it.

"Damien, take her to the car," Cameron said, never moving his gaze off the man he still held. I glanced to the side, seeing Damien, not sure where he'd come from.

"Let's go," Damien said, grabbing my arm, steering me out of the room, down the hall, and out the front door.

The limo was already waiting at the bottom of the steps. Damien opened the back door for me and gently pushed me inside. I don't know how long I sat there, my palms damp, my heart in my throat.

Finally the door opened again, and I saw Damien

hand Cameron a white rag. Cameron slipped in, his focus on his knuckles. That's when I saw the blood covering them. I lifted my gaze to his white shirt, seeing the splatters of red along the stark light color.

"Did you kill him?" I asked softly, almost frightened to know the answer. He didn't respond me right away, just continued to clean his hands off. I looked out my window, not expecting a response. This was Cameron, after all.

"Whether I did or didn't isn't the point."

I glanced at him after he spoke. "Isn't it?"

He looked at me then, his face hidden partially by the shadows, his expression void.

"No."

I slowly inhaled, not sure if I should push this. I wanted to, wanted to see what he was thinking about, what was going on in his head. I wanted to learn about him, know what made him tick. But I also knew Cameron was a mystery, didn't let people in, and I doubted even if he trusted them.

"But I didn't kill him, even if I should have." He stared me right in the eyes. "Make no mistake, Sofia. I wanted to rip his balls off and shove them down his throat for even thinking he could look at you." This draft of frigid air slammed into me. "The fact he touched you..." He shook his head slowly. "If he wasn't who he was, and a man I need alive for business purposes, I would have fucking gutted him."

I breathed in and out hard and fast, his words like a knife, sharp, deadly.

"And no one would have fucking stopped me." And then this expression covered his face, this hard, cold look that I felt to my bones. It was reflected at me. And then, just as fast as it had shown up, he masked it.

Cameron turned and looked out the window, and I did the same. I watched the scenery pass us by, not sure what the sudden change in him was. He seemed angry. Was he blaming this on me?

Why does it matter? In a few days I'll be gone—all of this behind me, my life in front of me.

But that felt so empty.

19

The final day

He'd kept his distance, made me feel isolated. I was starting to feel, to think, this had more to do with his emotions than the fact that he didn't want me.

I found myself moving through the house, running my fingers along the smooth wood, taking in the desolate, dark pictures. The man I cared about, had fallen for during my short time here, was more of an enigma than anything else.

He'd been beaten as a child, given away as if he were nothing. He'd fought to survive...literally, and here he was now, standing tall, above everyone else. Although my life, childhood, hadn't been this bottomless pit like he'd experienced, I did know the darkness he felt, even if it wasn't nearly to the extent he did.

I found myself in front of the bird painting, staring at the mouth, the bleak eyes. I felt for Cameron, wanted to be the one who comforted him, shared in his pain. But a man like him, one who had been through so much, hid what he needed. He wasn't normal in the sense that he needed, or wanted, comfort.

The way he got rid of that darkness, that hardness and hatred, was through rough contact and violence. He'd always be like that, and I accepted it. I accepted him.

I found myself moving away from the picture and back to the room. I'd be leaving tomorrow, saying goodbye to all of this, to Cameron. God, that hurt, made my chest ache. I rubbed it, right over my heart.

When I pushed the bedroom door open, I froze, seeing Cameron over by the window. His big body kept the curtain to the side as he stared out. There was a glass in his hand, presumably alcohol in it.

"Come in and shut the door," he said, his voice soft, low.

I did as he said, but as soon as the door was shut, I felt like I was trapped, no way to escape, no real reason I would want to.

"Come here."

I moved closer, feeling the air getting sucked out of my lungs, feeling the room grow hotter, everything becoming tighter. He stayed by the window, his focus on whatever was outside. It was dark, but there were lights on, golden illumination covering the manicured ground.

"I told you about my life." He turned. "In a way, I suppose." He took a small drink from his glass. "Beaten as a child, sold off to earn money for people who thought of us as nothing more than a commodity, a paycheck." He finished off the drink and set the now empty glass on the windowsill. "And no amount of tattoos can cover up the lasting impression they had on me, or what I went through." He advanced, one step, making me feel smaller, weaker. "And after a while I thrived on the pain, on getting it and hitting back." He grinned, and it was fucking frightening. "That's the type of man you allow in your bed, between your thighs." He was an inch from me now, the scent of alcohol making me drunk. "That's the man that you've grown to care about." He said that last part so low, so deep, I felt it to my marrow. "And you do care for me," he said as if he knew that with certainty.

"The man I've grown to care about..." I was saying it more to myself than asking it as a question, but the truth was between us. He knew it. I knew it. And there was no point in lying.

"Have you not grown to care for me?" He reached out, grabbed a lock of my hair, and rubbed it between his fingers.

I didn't answer. I couldn't right now anyway.

He kept rubbing my hair. "Like a distant memory," he whispered, almost to himself. But as soon as he let that piece of hair go, this hard mask covered his face. "I've come to realize the weakness you are to me is far too dangerous." He looked into my eyes, this piercing, soul-catching expression. "It's not what I want or need."

He turned, but I grabbed his hand, a bold gesture. He looked over his shoulder, down at my hand, his focus severe. "Don't you fucking see?" he said, his voice low, dangerous...deadly. "You are here for my pleasure, nothing more." He gave this humorous, scary laugh. "What did you think would happen, little girl?"

I didn't speak, not because I didn't want to, but because I didn't know what to say, how to respond. I didn't know how to be honest with him. I wasn't going to let his words affect me, wasn't going to let him try and push me away. At least not before I told him I cared for him, wanted him.

"I do care about you." And then, right in front of me, I saw that wall shifting, breaking down, being exposed to me.

He turned fully around to face me, that wall still breaking down. And then, before I knew what was going on, he pulled me in close. His anger was right there at the surface, and the internal war he fought was clear. He held my body to his, the stiffness of his erection pressing into my belly.

Would tonight be rough? Would he take me for the last time in the totally demented way he'd always told me about, threatened he could do to me? Sure, he'd been on the rougher side when he'd taken me, but he'd held me afterward and stroked my skin when he thought I was sleeping.

The feeling of his hand on my head, stroking my hair, gentle, caressing sweeps down the length, had me wishing for more time. I wished things could be different. I wished this could be permanent.

He took me to bed then, laying me down softly, being so gentle it almost brought tears to my eyes. This was not a side I'd ever seen in Cameron before.

He took my clothes off, his hands soft, sweet even. The kisses, licks, and nibbles made me think of this as a good-bye, that one moment where he was mine and I was his. Once we were naked, his body on top of mine, his hard cock nestled right between my thighs, I was the one who reached down. I was the one who grabbed his dick, placed the tip at my entrance, and urged him to penetrate me.

I wanted to feel him deep in my body, stretching me in the way he always did. This was our last time, and although I hated it, wanted to demand he accept what was going on, admit he had feelings for me, I kept my mouth shut.

And then he did push into me, rocked back and forth, kept his hand on my throat, and took control. He was gentle, not rushing it, and a part of me knew he wanted it to last. A part of me knew he wanted me to stay, even if he didn't say the words, even if he wouldn't.

I let him fill me up, claim me, make me understand I was the only woman, the one who held his attention. It didn't matter what tomorrow held. In this moment I didn't care about anything but being with him.

And when we both found that completion, and he filled me up in the most basic of senses, he pulled out and lay beside me. He held me, pushed my hair from my face, and stared into my eyes. The tattoos, his scars, the life he'd led and the one he continued to lead, didn't mean anything in that moment. It was just a man and a woman.

It was just us.

I pulled back and looked at him. This mask was on his face once more, that darkness that recognized me so well, that related to me like the other half of my soul.

"Maybe I don't have to leave." I didn't know if he'd answer, didn't know if he'd react. He was silent, still—his hand still on my body, his focus still on me. And then his jaw hardened, his eyes went flat, and I knew, just *knew*, come morning, he wouldn't be in the bed with me. Whatever internal battle he was dealing with was not something I would be allowed to witness.

I don't know if that broke my heart or reminded me that this was exactly who I'd fallen in love with.

———

The next morning

I SLOWLY OPENED MY EYES, the sun coming through the partially opened blinds washing over me, an invisible blanket of heat, comfort. I was alone in bed. I knew that without even turning and looking at Cameron's side. This longing took place right in the center of my chest, this pressure, this emptiness.

I would go home today, or whatever my shitty apartment could be called.

A part of me hoped Cameron would force me to stay, make me his prisoner...only his. I knew I wasn't the only one who felt this way, clutching at this feeling of being alive, of not being alone anymore. He was hard in all ways, indifferent, cold. But when he looked at me, I saw something shift. I felt it in him, this wave crashing to the surface, brutal, violent almost, but also so beautiful.

I didn't want to move, just wanted to let the situation filter over me, consume me, take me under until I was one with it. But the sound of the door opening had me glancing over, hoping, wishing it was Cameron. I wanted him to tell me I was his, only his, that he wouldn't let me go. I wanted to be his prisoner. I wanted to be the woman he turned to in order to find that pleasure.

I wanted to be his outlet, because in the end that's who and what he was to me. I knew things wouldn't be the same without him in my life, giving me that beautiful torment, that painful pleasure.

But it was the maid, her focus on the ground, her hair in a severe bun. She set a tray on the end of the bed, not speaking to me, and turned to leave. The door had only been shut for a moment or two before there was another knock. I pushed myself up on the bed and brought the sheet to my chin. I was naked, my body pleasantly sore, my inner thighs sticky from Cameron's release just last night. There was another knock, and then I finally called out for them to enter.

Damien pushed the door open, his focus trained on my face before he glanced down at the ground. "Cameron has business to attend to, but he instructed me to inform you that after breakfast, and once you're dressed, I'll take you wherever you want to go."

God, my throat was so dry, and this anxiety started to consume me, pulling me further under, making me feel uncomfortable. "I won't see him before I leave?"

I hated that I felt so small, so vulnerable right now. I loathed the fact that Cameron made me feel like this and was either too afraid or too much of a bastard to face me himself. I knew I wasn't hiding my emotions well, knew I was glaring. But Damien, being the stone statue he was, said nothing.

"I'll be downstairs waiting when you're ready." He looked at me, and if he was the type of man to show any emotion, I might have thought he felt sorry for me. Yeah, I felt sorry for me too. I'd let my emotions get the best of me, allowed them to hold on tight and not let go.

And then he left me alone, and I sat there staring at the tray of food. I would not let this control me. I couldn't, because if I did, there would be no one there to help me out of the hole when it was all said and done.

I sat alone in the back of the car, the scent of leather filling my head, but there was also the slight aroma of the cologne Cameron wore. I hadn't seen him when I left the room and met Damien downstairs, but then again, I hadn't expected to. He was a coward, if a killer could be one. He'd fucked me last night, even held me as I fell asleep, but come morning he'd been gone. He hadn't even given me the decency or respect to say good-bye.

We entered the city and I stared out the window, watching the buildings pass by, seeing the people oblivious to anything that wasn't right in front of them. I assumed Damien was taking me back to the apartment building, but I didn't want to go there.

"Stop," I said loudly enough I was sure Damien heard. "Pull in here." He didn't question me, just pulled into the driveway and found a parking spot. For a second I stared at the run-down motel, watching the few people loiter on the top balcony, their cigarettes hanging from their mouths, their hair and clothes greasy. I was sure drug deals, even some prostitution went on here. Before I could get out, Damien was climbing out of the car and opening the back door for me.

I was thankful he kept his mouth shut, didn't hassle me on the shithole place I wanted to be dropped off at. But the little I had was at the apartment, a place I didn't want to go back to, but would probably end up having to in order to at least survive until the next day.

"This is for you." Damien handed me a small black bag. "Inside you'll find a few changes of clothes from your stay at the house, some money to allow you to leave the city, and this." He gave me a small slip of paper. A number was written on it, and I wondered if it was Cameron's or Damien's. I didn't ask.

"You're free, safe, and have enough money in that bag to start a life someplace else, someplace less shitty." I stared at the number, listening to Damien's voice, thinking about Cameron.

"He didn't want to say good-bye to me," I found myself saying, not sure if I was asking myself or Damien.

"He had business to attend to."

I glanced up at Damien then. I knew I was just a payment, a debt owed because Cameron had helped me, solved my problem. It was what it was, although I hated the fact I couldn't see him. I fucking hated the fact I found myself falling for my dark protector, the man willing to kill to make sure I was okay.

"If you're in trouble, you call that number and someone will be there."

Instead of saying something, making a fool out of myself, I just nodded.

I took a step back, watched Damien get into the car, and as he drove away I couldn't help but take in a stuttering breath. I realized in that moment that before

Cameron I'd just been surviving. With him I'd been living. But he'd made his point clear, stayed away, took from me what he wanted, and because of my need to survive, to be a fighter, I turned away from the disappearing car, faced the motel, and tried to think about the future.

I wouldn't lie...it looked pretty damn dark.

20

One week later

I wanted to think that the dark SUVs I'd seen were Cameron looking out for me, hiding inside, watching me, unable to just ignore what we'd shared for those fourteen days. But I wasn't such a fool to think I meant more than a warm hole to relieve himself in.

No, it was more than that. I was his, only his. He made that clear at the party, when he touched me, stroked me from the inside out. He told me as much when he whispered filthy words in my ear as he thrust deep and hard into my body.

I'd found myself back at the shitty apartment, packing up what little I had owned. There wasn't much I wanted to take with me, nothing of great value or importance. But for this last week I'd been trying to push forward, to forget about everything and anything that had to do with Cameron, with my stay in his home. I couldn't shake him, couldn't get rid of the image of him, of the memory of how he felt when he touched me.

I shoved the last piece of clothing into my backpack, stepped back, and stared at it on my bed. The small black bag Damien had given me before he left sat beside it, the money and phone number within it. Truth was I'd hoped Cameron would come for me, would demand I go with him, stay with him...never leave. And I wouldn't have.

I wanted him, desired that free feeling I had, that moment of bliss where I wasn't wondering where I was going, where I was headed. Truth was I didn't know where I was going, not even now, not even with a bag full of money and an empty road ahead of me. I heard the honk of the taxi I'd called downstairs waiting for me, and I grabbed my things and headed outside. But as I stood there, staring at the idling yellow car, the rust around the edges dark, almost like blood under the setting sun, the worry and pain claimed me. I rubbed at my chest, the idea of leaving, of not telling Cameron what I wanted, who I wanted, wearing down on me so heavily I couldn't even breathe.

"You coming or what?" the taxi driver shouted out the open passenger window. I took a step toward it, but froze, finding myself shaking my head. I couldn't leave without at least telling Cameron how I felt, how he made me feel.

"No," I whispered, but when I heard the driver curse, I

knew he'd heard me just fine. He sped off, his tires screeching out, the name he'd called me right before he took off ringing in my head. I grabbed the cheap pay-for-minutes phone out of my backpack, took the slip of paper out as well, and stared at both of them. I knew that I should have just left, said good-bye to those two weeks, to the shit life I'd allowed myself to live. But I was still here and wanting to be truthful for once in my life.

If he wanted me, wouldn't he have stayed, made me be with him? If he craved me the way I do him, wouldn't he have come for me by now? Maybe he wants nothing to do with me. Was I just a convenience, a person to find his pleasure in?

Or could he be doing this, staying away, to protect me?

It was that latter thought, the little nagging in the back of my head, that had me dialing the number Damien had given me. I stood there, feeling cold all of a sudden, nervous, my hands shaking, my breath coming out hard and fast. And when the ringing stopped, I swore my heart did too.

"I need Cameron," I said, not sure what the future held in me making this decision, but wanting to find out either way. I needed to.

I stayed in front of my apartment building, the man on the other end not a voice I recognized. But he'd told me to stay put, that they knew where I was, and someone would come here to pick me up. I didn't exactly know what my problem was, and for all I knew they assumed it was bad if I was calling them. But I'd have to be honest, tell them there was no "problem," not in the sense they were probably thinking.

I had to see Cameron again, even if this was the last, the only time. I had to admit my feelings, that I felt lost without him, that being his, letting him consume me in the way he had, was what I needed in my life. I wanted to think that I was prepared if he pushed me aside, that he might cut me deep with his words, but truth was I probably wasn't.

It had been ten minutes since I'd made the call, and I saw a dark SUV turn the corner and come my way. My heart raced at the sight of it, and I knew my anticipation and nervousness might have been considered fear by looking at me. The vehicle came to a stop beside the curb in front of me, and the driver's side door opened. I watched Damien come around, his focus intense on me. I also noticed he kept scanning the area. He opened the back door for me, and I saw long, muscular legs covered in expensive material come into view.

Cameron.

I climbed into the back of the SUV, the door shutting behind me, my eyes needing to adjust to the change in light. And when they did I stared at Cameron, who sat beside me. He stared at me, his dark gaze locked on me, the hairs on the back of my neck standing on end.

"Take us to the property, Damien," Cameron said without breaking his focus on me. The car started moving, and I settled back. I didn't know what property he was referring to, but I didn't really want to do this with an audience.

It was me who ended up breaking the eye contact and looking out the window. I don't know how long we drove for, but it was done in silence, the air thick, the temperature hot. Maybe twenty minutes or so later we finally pulled onto a dirt road, staying on that for another ten minutes, and then stopping. The headlights illuminated the dilapidated house that stood in the distance, trees sporadically around the open property.

"Where are we?" When he didn't respond, I glanced at him.

"A piece of property I own. I come out here to meet with less than superior clients at times. I need this for privacy."

Yeah, I could see that. It was deserted, out in the middle of nowhere, and I had to assume if someone needed to use a gun, there would be no one around to hear it.

"You said you're in trouble." He didn't phrase it like a question. I glanced at Damien on instinct, because truthfully I wanted this to be a private conversation between Cameron and me.

"Give us a moment alone, Damien," Cameron finally said, but he was looking at me again. A second later Damien was out of the car. Cameron lifted an eyebrow, clearly waiting for me to speak.

"I'm not in trouble." I looked down at my hands. They

were in my lap, and I realized I was nervously picking at my shirt. I looked back at him again. "At least not in the way you are probably assuming."

"I know," he said, and a part of me wasn't really shocked he knew that. Cameron pretty much knew everything.

"You knew?" I found myself asking.

The look he gave me was indifferent. "You think I didn't know what you were doing, where you were, or if you were safe?"

I shifted, feeling the weight of his gaze on me, knowing he could read me with just a look.

"I knew, Sofia."

I twisted my hands together, swallowing roughly. "I assumed you didn't care." This was really not how I'd seen this conversation going. For a second we didn't speak, but everything seemed so loud, so intense.

"Why didn't you say good-bye? Why didn't you see me before I left?" I might as well lay it all out, because that was the whole reason I'd called him. "Did I mean nothing to you?" My voice was whisper soft, my emotions threatening to come forth. I wouldn't let them though. I wouldn't let them control me, wouldn't let Cameron see them. He looked away from me, out the window, and for long seconds stayed like that. I wanted to say something, anything, but my mouth was suddenly dry, and the words didn't want to form.

"I wanted to see you," he finally said, breaking that

thick silence and making my ears ring with awareness. "But watching you leave was too hard. If I'd been there, seeing you get into that car, I'd have pulled you away and demanded you stay." He looked at me then. My heart was beating so hard it hurt. "I wanted to keep you as mine, to have you close, care for you. But even a bastard like me knows my world is too toxic for you, Sofia." Even though his words held so much meaning, he kept his cool composure.

"You saw where I came from, where my life was," I whispered.

He reached out, and for a second I thought he'd pull me close, say fuck it all, and tell me I was his. Instead he pushed a strand of my hair away, his finger brushing along my cheek, a shiver working its way through my body.

"All the materialistic things are easy to give you, Sofia. It's the happily ever after I can't offer."

I shifted to face him fully. "I don't want a happily ever after." I shook my head. "I don't want the fairy tale."

"Tell me what it is you want, what I can give you." He shifted slightly too, his big body facing me now. "Because mayhem and bloodshed rule my world." He was the one to slowly shake his head now. "As much as I want you chained to my side, only mine, I can't be a motherfucker and say that's what's right for you, safe for you."

He held my gaze with his own, that focus speaking so

loudly. Seconds ticked by, and I wanted to tell him so much more, explain how I felt, what he did to me.

"I want to keep you safe from my world...from *me*, Sofia."

I reached out to him, not stopping myself, not able to help myself. "Don't you see, it's your world that I want? I need everything and anything that makes up Cameron Ashton. It's your darkness that calls to me, that makes me feel alive, makes me yearn for more." I was crying now, and Cameron reached out to smooth his thumb over my cheek, collecting the tear. He brought it to his mouth and sucked the droplet off, focusing on me. Always on me.

"You make me cry because I'm happy." I finally broke up the silence.

"I don't think I've ever tasted your tears when you've been happy," he said softly. He had, even if he didn't realize it.

"You make me happy," I said honestly, not about to deny how I felt anymore. I wasn't going to lie, wasn't going to hide. "And being without you and not feeling that passion, darkness...freedom, is not something I want to experience, Cameron." I braced myself for the rejection, because even if he did want me, he was a strong-willed man. But before I could say something else, maybe repeat how much he meant to me, how much I needed him in my life, he had me pulled onto his lap. His arms were around me, holding me painfully tight.

"You're not afraid, not terrified of the man I am, the corruption I'll smother you with?"

I rested my head on his shoulder, hearing his breath move along my ear, smelling the manly scent of him that surrounded me, and wanting nothing more than to stay in this moment forever.

"Would you have come for me?" I didn't know if I wanted to know the answer.

He stroked my back, running his hands up and down, soothing me, making me feel whole.

"It was hard not making you stay with me, but for once in my life I tried to be the good guy. I tried to let you go free." He pulled me back and looked into my face. "But honestly, yes, I would have." He cupped the side of my face, the heat from his body like fire on my skin. "I would have crushed anyone and made a bridge out of their bodies just to get to you."

My heart stuttered in my chest.

"You're sure you want this? Because if so I'm really not fucking letting go."

For the first time in my life I wasn't afraid of anything. "I'm sure."

He crushed me to him, and I let that darkness fill me, match my own, grab on to it and not let go.

EPILOGUE

Life has a funny way of working out, of moving forward when you think it has stopped, stuck in the past. I hadn't known what life was like, not truly, not fully, until Cameron opened me up, saw inside, let me see who I really was. Maybe I would have found out what I liked, how I wanted to spread my wings and fly, experience life in my own way, sooner or later. Maybe I didn't need a man who shared the same darkness I did to know I wasn't broken, wasn't ruined.

Maybe it took a man who was just as scuffed up as me to know I wasn't alone.

Even as a year had passed, my life revolving on my terms, on my time, I still felt like that lost girl. And when I saw Cameron, felt his hands on me, heard the words of his possession, of his dark love, then I felt alive. I wasn't a victim, not unless I made myself one.

Never again.

I sat behind Cameron's desk at the estate, going over the club paperwork, the finances, the employment history. I was in charge of helping Damien hire on new staff, vetting them out, making sure they could be trusted, even if they'd just be delivering drinks to customers. It was what I wanted to do, be a part of something bigger. It might not be the most prestigious job, a path I saw myself doing, but it allowed me to be near the man I loved, and earn my own money—even if Cameron insisted on taking care of me in all ways.

The sound of the door opening had me glancing up. Damien stood in the doorway, his hands behind him, his body ramrod straight. "He's here."

Just then my cell rang, and I picked it up and saw Cameron's number flash along the screen. As if on instinct my body warmed, became soft, and everything in me was alive with awareness...anticipation.

"You're ready, baby?"

His deep voice pierced right through me, and I glanced at Damien, feeling my face heat, my body reacting to the sound of Cameron's voice.

"Yes." I disconnected the call, stood, and smoothed my hands down the evening gown Cameron had sent to the house for me to wear. I turned and faced the window, seeing the gleam of his black Mercedes coming up the drive, the sun glinting off the exterior, the windows tinted so I wasn't able to see him.

He was taking me out, and although Cameron never did anything normal, and this wouldn't be a dinner and chick-flick kind of night, he made sure each and every second we spent together was intimate and special. At least that's how he made me feel.

I left the room when the Mercedes came to a stop. I felt Damien follow behind, his big body always a constant. Over the last year, and honestly well before I was even in this situation, in this relationship with Cameron, Damien had always been there. He was the silent enforcer, the man who looked after me, made sure Cameron had his back watched at all times. He was a part of us in his own way, and the truth was if he wasn't around, I would feel this loss. It was strange, but that was my world now.

I opened the front door and stepped outside, the sun already set, the moon high, and the lights of the estate in full bloom. My heart started beating even harder, even faster. Damien was already moving toward the back of the Mercedes, and when he opened the door and Cameron stepped out, that puzzle piece fit right back in place inside of me.

For a second Cameron and Damien stood by the car and spoke softly. I didn't need to know what they said, didn't need to wonder if there was shady back-alley shit going down. This was the life I'd agreed to, the life I wanted to have for my own. Cameron was the man I wanted by my side.

"Leave us," Cameron said to Damien, and also to the driver, who I hadn't noticed get out of the car until now. When it was just Cameron and me, the familiar heat I felt with Cameron filled me. "Come here," he commanded, his voice smooth yet hard. I moved toward him, and once I was close enough he could reach out and touch me, he did just that. I was in Cameron's arms seconds later, the heels I wore not even having me come up to his chin. He was strong where I was fragile. He was masculine where I was feminine.

He was the vast openness where I was the darkness. He swallowed me whole without even trying, without even needing to.

"I've rented out the theater. It'll be us. Only us."

"Just the way you like it," I said and tipped my head back to look at him. He didn't smile, didn't really show me any emotion, but he didn't need to. The way he looked at me, that possession in his eyes, told me all I needed to know. I was his world.

"I like to keep you all to myself. Always." He held me tighter. Cameron would never be called sweet or gentle, not in the traditional sense. But that's not why I loved him, not why I came back and stayed with him. I did so because he gave me what I needed, craved.

And I gave him what he needed.

Before Cameron I was a bird with clipped wings, living in a rusted cage, the door locked, the key thrown away. But now I flew high, experienced the world, let my wings spread out, and the wind rush over me.

"What do you see when you look at me?" I asked, staring into his eyes, seeing that darkness focused on me. With his hands on my face, his body pressed tightly to mine, I felt like I'd never fall.

"Vastness," he said softly. "You're my ocean, Sofia. I can't see anything else but you."

BONUS EPILOGUE

Cameron

Two years later

For two years I'd kept Sofia as mine, made sure she was protected, the darkness I harbored inside making sure she was safe. The sweet sounds coming from the other room had me moving closer, my heart racing, my thoughts turbulent.

The type of man I was—am—ensured that I never saw myself having a woman, a wife or mother of my child. But over the last couple of years I'd gotten all of that and more. I was still a hardcore motherfucker, dealt with illegal holdings, made sure that anyone who thought to cross me knew exactly the wrath I'd inflict on them.

But with Sofia and the innocent child she'd given me, I thought I would have softened, bended to the life that a motherfucker like me didn't deserve to have.

But I had become even more ruthless, even more dangerous. They were my life, and keeping them safe and happy was my priority.

I stopped in the doorway of the nursery, the baby pink and white décor so soft and unlike the possessions I had in this home. It was the one ray of light in this barren structure, save for the woman who held my heart above all others. I could see the lights shining outside, the body-guards patrolling the grounds. They were here twenty-four-seven, always ensuring no one came onto the property.

I turned my attention back to Sofia, who held our three-month-old daughter. For long minutes, all I did was watch them, knowing that even a bastard like me could be granted the gift of happiness. Sofia hummed to Sasha, and after a few seconds our daughter started to sleep. She held the baby for long minutes after that, running her fingers through the thick tuft of dark hair atop her head, down the bridge of her tiny nose, and tracing her little pink lips.

I stood there until Sofia put the baby down in the crib, stared down at the little person we'd created, and finally turned toward me. She seemed surprised to see me standing there, but the smile she gave me lit up the entire fucking room.

"Come here," I said softly, but the harshness in my voice was clear. I was hard for my woman, and even though I should have turned away and let her be, let her body heal from the last raw, hard fucking I'd given her just the night before, I needed her now.

She came to me instantly and I held her close, my hand on the roundness of her ass, my other palm cupping the back of her head. I kept her close as I stared at the crib where our child slept.

Sasha hadn't been planned, but that didn't mean she wasn't a blessing or wanted. I couldn't even picture my darkened, hardened life without her in it. Before my daughter was born, Sofia was what made my world bright. Now that the baby was here it was both of my girls that made me want to be a better man, even if I never would be.

I closed my eyes and inhaled the sweet, intoxicating scent of Sofia. My dick got hard, digging into her belly, demanding to be buried deep in her pretty, tight cunt.

"I want you," she said and pulled back to look up into my face.

I ground my cock into her belly, loving the little sound she made. We left the nursery and went into our bedroom. She moved over to the bed, stripped without me prompting her, and stood there waiting for me to devour her.

I let my gaze slide down her body, loving the curves she'd gotten after giving birth. She was gorgeous and mine, and my handprints would look beautiful on her pale flesh. I kept moving my gaze down until I reached her pussy, free of any hair, shaved because I wanted her smooth for when I had my mouth on her.

Sofia was mine, and every part of her body belonged to me. I showed her every day how true that was, and would never stop showing her until I took my last breath.

Her breathing was changing slightly, increasing, becoming harder, faster with her arousal. Her breasts rose and fell, her nipples hard, the tips a dusky rose.

"How wet are you for me?" I said on a low, deep voice, and felt my own desire rising higher.

"So wet."

"Then get on the bed and spread wide for me, show me how primed you are for my cock."

She got on the bed, her feet flat on the mattress, her pussy on clear display. I got undressed and immediately grabbed my cock. I stroked myself from root to tip, felt the pre-cum start to form, and used it for lubrication. I moved closer to her and stopped when I reached the edge of the bed. For long seconds all I did was stare at her as I masturbated, gave her a little show so she could see exactly how worked up I was, how much I wanted her.

Her cunt was red and swollen, and so fucking wet for me. My dick would slide right in, spread her wide, stretch her good. "Spread your legs even wider for me, Sofia."

She made a small noise, and my dick hardened even more. I didn't bother stopping myself from getting on my knees between her splayed thighs and slipping my fingers through her folds, coating the digits with her cream. I then lifted them to my mouth and sucked them clean as she watched me. I was starved for her in every way imaginable. And then I had my face buried between her legs. I licked and sucked, swallowed her arousal, and growled for more. The moans that came from her fueled my dark desire.

I forced myself to pull away from her pretty pussy, but had a finger lodged in her tight, wet and hot body a second later. I pumped that finger in and out of her and then added another one. I scissored the digits, stretching her good and hard, and she moaned for me, squirming under my touch.

I needed this, needed her in all ways.

"You're mine." I couldn't control myself any longer. I removed my fingers from her body, took her chin in a firm hold, and kissed her hard, making her taste herself on my lips and tongue.

"I need you now," she begged, pleading for more.

She was mine, and I might own her body, but she owned every single fucking part of me. I positioned myself so my cockhead was at her pussy hole and slid in without waiting. I had a firm hold on her waist, and knew I would leave bruises on her creamy flesh. But I needed to see those marks.

The feeling of pushing into her, feeling her clench around my cock and her moaning out my name, nearly had me coming right then and there. My balls drew up tight from my release rising to the surface. "Give it all to me."

She mewled from the pleasure. The air left me harshly when she squeezed her pussy muscles around me.

"You feel so fucking good." I moved in and out of her hard and fiercely, picking up my pace, slamming my hips against hers. I leaned back and watched as my cock tunneled in and out of her slick, soaked pussy.

I was going to come, but first I wanted her getting off. I started pumping in and out of her faster, and moved my hand between us, rubbing my thumb along her clit. "Come for me, Sofia." And then I felt the first ripple of her orgasm move along my shaft.

"Oh. God, yes," she cried out long and hard.

This was what I wanted, her sweet surrender. And as she came for me I let myself go over the edge right along with her. The groan that came from me was harsh, guttural. I filled her up, marking her and claiming every fucking part of her. Only when my pleasure dimmed did I pull out of her and collapse on the bed beside her.

Sofia breathed out heavily and I pulled her close to me, our bodies sweaty, sated.

I still had darkness inside of me, but it was one that Sofia owned.

She was the only one that could tame me.

"I love you," Sofia said softly, and I felt this low growl

leave me, contentment and happiness filling my black-ened heart.

"I love you, too, so fucking much it consumes me."

I might never be a knight in white armor for her, sweeping in and destroying the bad guy, but I could be the fucking devil who took care of any motherfucker who crossed her.

I could still give her that happily ever after, even if it was by the light of the moon instead of the brightness of the sun.

The End

NEWSLETTER

Want to know when Jenika has book related news, and giveaways, and free books?

You can get all of that and more by following the link below!

————

Sign Up Here: http://eepurl.com/ce7yS-/

————

Want your very own Real Man? Check out the series
HERE: http://amzn.to/2szRFss

WANT MORE?

Find all of Jenika's dirty, sweet, and everything in-between books here:

http://www.jenikasnow.com/bookshelf

EXCERPT: A BEAUTIFUL PRISON

A BEAUTIUL PRISON

By Jenika Snow

www.JenikaSnow.com

Jenika_Snow@Yahoo.com

First E-book Publication: March 2014

Cover design by Jay Aheer

Copyright © 2014 Jenika Snow

ALL RIGHTS RESERVED: The unauthorized reproduction, transmission, or distribution of any part of this copyrighted work is illegal. Criminal copyright infringement is investigated by the FBI and is punishable by up to 5 years in federal prison and a fine of $250,000.

This literary work is fiction. Any name, places, characters and incidents are the product of the author's imagination. Any resemblance to actual persons, living or dead, events or establishments is solely coincidental.

Please respect the author and do not participate in or encourage piracy of copyrighted materials that would violate the author's rights.

Ruby Jacobson wanted a new life, but it seemed fate gave her a twisted version of it.

Gavin Darris has always desired the darker pleasures in life. Normally not one to purchase his playthings, he needed a woman who would bend to his will, and derive pleasure from it, too.

He saw Ruby, one of the many women for sale, and he wanted her as his. She had a fire in her eyes and a determination not to yield. She looked like a fighter and was exactly what he wanted.

He was ruthless in what he wanted, and what he wanted was Ruby.

The dark desires Ruby has always felt inside of her are about to be tempted. She should hate Gavin and fear everything he represents, but she can't deny that her body aches for his touch. He tells her she is his; that he owns every part of her, and everything inside of her knows that is the truth.

Faced with the ultimate decision, Ruby must choose to escape and gain her freedom, or stay with Gavin, the monster whose delicious punishment makes her yearn for more.

Both are frightening.

PREFACE

She was his.

Irrevocably. Undeniably.

He knew this as soon as he saw her bound on the stage. He needed to possess her, own her, and make sure she knew that he was the one that held all the power. She was his property now, whether she accepted that or not. She would soon come to realize that there was no escape.

He had bought her, picked her from all the other women that had been taken and sold like nothing more than inanimate objects. However, she wasn't just an object. She was *his* to do with as he pleased.

She looked at him with fear, but she hadn't felt real fear yet. He was a monster, the kind that she had probably dreamt about as a child, prayed she would never meet, and one that now owned her.

She would run, there was no doubt about that, but

what she would soon realize was he wanted her to. He reveled in the chase, and when he caught her, he'd make her pay with her body until she gave him every part of herself.

He was a sadist, and with each passing day, she would realize that she was his perfect masochist.

1

It was sweet, beautiful pain that filled her mind, washed through her, and had her needy for more. She wanted to stay here forever, in this dream that seemed to haunt her nightly. However, she couldn't really say it haunted her, not when she prayed for the sweet release it brought her every night before she closed her eyes.

Disgust and shame filled her each morning when she reflected on those dreams. For pain *with* pleasure wasn't "normal," right? It made no difference because it was only in her dreams that she would allow these dark desires to control her. She enjoyed the idea of marks on her flesh, a hand on her throat, slowly tightening until darkness threatened to take her away. Only in her dreams could she ever allow herself that moment of depravity.

An outraged scream and the sound of something

shattering had Ruby slowly opening her eyes. She blinked a few times, but otherwise stayed in the bed, her comforter that smelled faintly of mold pulled up to her chin, and stared at the ceiling. It was off-white, but riddled with brown stains.

Her mother yelled something nasty and ugly, presumably at her boyfriend. Ruby thought his name was Buck, or maybe it was Chuck. She didn't really know or care since there seemed to be a new one every week. With her graduation already past, it was finally time for her to leave. She had been thinking about this moment for years and time had finally come.

Ruby was going to leave this shitty city behind her, forget about the ugliness that surrounded her every single day, and start over. She didn't even have a set plan, but she didn't need one because she just didn't care. The idea of spending one more moment surrounded by the failings of her upbringing was enough to push her out the door.

She'd work things out when she got to Fort Hampton. Maybe she would fail and feel just as misplaced as she did right now, but she wouldn't know unless she tried. If she stayed here another moment longer, she knew she wouldn't survive.

Her mind felt like it was deteriorating with every harsh comment that left her mother's mouth and with every inhalation of this smog-filled air. With a trailer to call home, a reputation as "trash" all through high school, and no friends, Ruby was used to feeling as if she didn't belong. Yes, she isolated herself, but she found that being alone was a much better existence.

The waste that surrounded her, the feelings of emptiness, and no self-worth was something Ruby knew, but not something she wanted. There was a big world out there, one that she could explore and hopefully, start to feel like she was finally living.

She pushed up on the bed and the comforter fell away from her body. She hadn't fallen asleep until well after midnight, courtesy of her mother and the boyfriend of the week having sex in the next room. The paper-thin walls did nothing to block out the sound of a banging headboard and the vile things the two said to each other. Scrubbing her hands over her face, she dropped them and exhaled.

She reached over and grabbed her cell. Flipping it open, she stared at the lit screen. It was only five-thirty in the morning and already the yelling had started. Tossing the cheap phone back on her scarred bedside table, she decided she'd rather be sitting at the bus stop than stay here one more minute. It was only a matter of time before her mother took out her anger on Ruby.

After she had her jeans on, she grabbed a T-shirt and slipped it over her head. Getting on her knees and reaching under her bed, she felt for the straps of her backpack and wrapped her fingers around it. Once she pulled it out, she reached inside for her ratty hoodie. It was ugly as hell, but well loved.

She grabbed the one-way ticket to Fort Hampton and moved her fingers over it. It was a fourteen-hour bus ride, and she had no idea what she would do once she got there, but anything was better than this. She tucked the ticket in the bag next to her money. Once she had her hoodie and her shoes on, she sat back on her bed.

It was sad that everything she owned fit into this bag. Clothes, the thousand dollars she had saved from working at the fast food place down the street, and a few personal items were all inside the confines of the canvas.

Although she had no definitive plans once she got to Fort Hampton, she had researched some cheap places she could stay. She had restaurant experience, well, fast food experience, but she was hoping to find something of that nature to do as soon as she got there. The thousand dollars she had wouldn't last her very long.

Standing and slinging her bag over her shoulders, she moved toward her door and waited a moment to see if there would be any more yelling.

She pulled it open as silently as she could and listened again. Should she have felt guilt over the fact she planned to leave without telling the woman that had given birth to her? Maybe she would if that woman had actually acted like a mother in the first place.

The lights were on, and she stepped out of her room shutting the door quietly behind her. If her mom was fighting with Buck/Chuck, she would already be in a foul mood. The sound of the TV was low, but she didn't let that distract her. Ruby kept her eyes averted to the ground and made her way toward the front door.

"And where the hell do you think you're going?" On instinct, Ruby stopped and looked over at Missy Jacobson, her mother and the woman who treated her like she shit on the bottom of her shoe.

She sat at the cracked, faded yellow Formica kitchen table, littered with cigarette burns. A bottle of whiskey in front of her, the glass beside it was nearly empty. The bags under her mom's eyes were dark, and it was clear she hadn't gone to bed yet. Missy lifted the cigarette she held to her mouth and inhaled deeply. She pulled it away and flicked the ash into the small aluminum tray beside the liquor bottle.

"You gonna answer me or stand there like a fucking idiot?" she said at the same time she exhaled all that smoke.

Ruby tightened her hold on one strap of her bag. "I have work early today." Telling her mom that she was leaving for good would only cause a fight, especially since Ruby had been giving part of her paycheck to Missy since she started working.

With this being her only home, it was either help keep this piece of shit trailer afloat or have her mom kick her out. Finishing school had been a priority for Ruby, so she sucked it up and told herself that as soon as she had her diploma she would be out of there. Today was that day, and Missy Jacobson wasn't going to ruin it.

"Is that right?" Missy took another puff from her cigarette and exhaled. "Then why you need that backpack? Flipping burgers and filling up Styrofoam cups doesn't require a lot of books."

"I have to go."

"I need money for rent."

Ruby stopped and looked over at her mom. "I just gave you some last week."

Missy shrugged. "What can I say? Keeping your big ass in this house costs money. There's electricity, water, rent. A lot of shit."

"I don't have any more." Missy narrowed her eyes.

"Girl, I put up with your ass prancing around here in your damn underwear, trying to tempt my men. You're fucking lucky I let you even live here. You're more damn trouble than you're worth." Ruby wasn't about to argue over the fact she sure as hell didn't prance around anywhere in just her underwear. In fact, she rarely came out of her room when she was home, not after one of her mother's boyfriends tried to touch her.

Missy poured herself another shot and tipped the glass back to her lips. Her eyes were glossy and red-rimmed, and Ruby knew she was drunk, probably had been since yesterday.

"I should have aborted your ass when I found out I was pregnant." Bile rose in Ruby's stomach. Even though nothing her mom said was sweet and loving, and was always vile in nature, it still hurt like hell.

"I'll bring you some money after work."

Missy leaned back in the seat. "You better or you can kiss your room goodbye."

Ruby stared at her mom for another second. "Bye."

Missy didn't even respond, just stared straight ahead, and smoked. Ruby felt no sadness in leaving. In fact, there was a very deep comfort in the knowledge that this was the last time she would step foot in this shithole.

Anything was better than this, including sleeping under a bridge, which might be a possibility once she reached Fort Hampton.

———

RUBY WRAPPED her arms around her middle when a gust of wind whipped by her. The sound of the approaching bus and her cramping stomach had woken her from a somewhat restless sleep. She had been at the bus station all day, sleeping off and on as best she could with the noise all around her.

She had only had a granola bar and a bottle of water since she left the trailer. She could have eaten something a bit more substantial, but she wanted to save every penny for Fort Hampton.

Straightening as the bus pulled to a stop, she noticed that several people lined up to get on the Greyhound. The smell of burning rubber from the bus braking and the exhaust filling the air around her had Ruby covering her mouth and nose with her hoodie. The door on the bus slid open and people inside started piling out.

When the last person stepped off the bus, it was a few minutes before anyone could get on as the attendants cleaned it. Ruby glanced at the people waiting to load. There were a few families with children in tow, some college-aged kids, and the occasional elderly person.

Ruby glanced along the row of people once more and her gaze stopped at one of the several benches that lined the side of the bus station. A man in a long black trench coat held a newspaper in his lap, his attention on her.

He didn't look very old, maybe in his early twenties, with brown hair slicked back from his face, and eyes that looked black and bottomless. There was a clear darkness inside of him, and even though they were several feet apart, Ruby felt a very uncomfortable sensation move along the length of her spine.

What she should have done was look away, but there was an invisible force keeping their gazes locked. She didn't know him, had never seen him before, but he made her feel like he could see into her soul, and knew every secret she held.

She quickly glanced away, tightened her hold on the backpack in her lap, and felt very uneasy all of a sudden. She still felt his stare boring into her, so she stood, needing to get on the bus and put some distance between them. Why did she have this sudden sense of wariness?

Maybe her situation had her on edge. The knowledge that she didn't know what her life would be like. That rationalization had her easing slightly because it seemed logical enough.

Ruby took her place in line and waited as everyone loaded onto the bus. Maybe she shouldn't have, but she found herself glancing at where the young man had been sitting. A breath left her, one that she hadn't realized she had been holding, when she saw he was no longer sitting there. Yes, she was overreacting, seeing things that weren't there because of the huge step she was taking.

Putting everything behind her, the life she'd led, the worry she'd felt since deciding to follow through with her plan, she handed the driver her ticket and climbed on the bus. There was a seat in the very back, and she moved down the aisle toward it. After taking her seat, she glanced out the window and watched the cars passing by on the street. *Well, this is finally it. You're leaving all this shit behind.* That had a smile curving her mouth even if she felt scared shitless.

A tingling on the back of her neck had her turning away from the window and glancing at the front of the bus, and instantly her heart started to beat faster. The guy in the dark duster climbed aboard. His head was downcast, but he lifted his eyes and looked right at her.

He took a seat a few rows in front of her, and she slid

down in her seat so she could no longer see him, pulling the hood of her sweatshirt over her head. Exhaustion settled heavily inside of her and she knew she wouldn't be able to keep her eyes open much longer. Blissful ignorance as she slept and dreams of a happier place sounded a lot better than her reality.

———

Available Now: https://amzn.to/2FlTegQ

Available Now: https://amzn.to/2r5vpV9

EXCERPT: HIS

HIS

Copyright © 2014 Jenika Snow

Published by Jenika Snow

www.JenikaSnow.com

Jenika_Snow@yahoo.com

Digital Edition

First E-book Publication: July 2014

Cover design by Jay Aheer

Editor: Kasi Alexander

ALL RIGHTS RESERVED: The unauthorized reproduction, transmission, or distribution of any part of this copyrighted work is illegal. Criminal copyright infringement is investigated by the FBI and is punishable by up to 5 years in federal prison and a fine of $250,000.

This literary work is fiction. Any name, places, characters and incidents are the product of the author's imagination. Any resemblance to actual persons, living or dead, events or establishments is solely coincidental.

Please respect the author and do not participate in or encourage piracy of copyrighted materials that would violate the author's rights.

Bethany Sterling came from a privileged family, one that believed in modern-day marriage arrangements. On the outside she played the part of the perfect daughter, but on the inside she was looking for another way out. She hid what she really wanted in life, because showing her dreams and aspirations was a weakness she couldn't afford to reveal.

As soon as Abe saw her he knew that he would go to any lengths to make her his. He was trained to be lethal, stealthy, and have no remorse in his actions. His dark needs take control of him until he was nothing more than a machine intent on following his plan.

Bethany finally got her wish for a new life, but it wasn't how she envisioned it. Now with Abe she realized that his need for her runs deep. He looked at her as if he owned not only her body, but her soul, as well. His possessiveness was something she should fear, but she was also compelled and attracted to him because of it.

It was those turbulent emotions pulling her in different directions that would have Bethany deciding how far she was willing to go.

WARNING: This is not a traditional love story. This

book does not end in the normal "happily ever after." There are no wedding bells at the end, no love being professed, or long walks on the beach. If that is the type of story you want this book probably isn't for you. This book is fiction and contains material readers may find offensive.

1

April 2014

Abe be watched her, had been watching her for over a year. Was it sick that he wanted her with this twisted obsession? No, it was sweet pleasure and anticipation that ran through his veins. Being so close to her and having the very depraved image of what he wanted to do to her playing through his mind was making him itchy. He needed her with him, needed to have her away from all of this saccharine falseness with the plastered-on smiles and the sick corruption.

On the outside he played the part, was the strict man that guarded her high-profile father. He was a trained killer, lethal in every way conceivable, and he wouldn't have had it any other way. Emotion clogged ultimate goals and caused the most skilled person to make mistakes. He had no emotions, and was not capable of the love and compassion that others drowned themselves in. What he had was determination and need, and all of it was centered on Bethany.

His training had been unorthodox, but the world was cruel and unforgiving and if he didn't take what he wanted then it would never be his. He was no military man, didn't have a Purple Heart for his bravery and being wounded at war. The questionable training he had received at a young age had molded him into the man he was today.

Deadly. Calculating. Intelligent.

Abe had been called all of those and more. But he was just a machine working toward the ultimate goal. And the end result would be the sweetest release he had ever had. Bethany would be his, and with his release would come hers. She also played the part that was expected of her, but he could see in her eyes she was trapped in a gold-gilded prison.

She wanted a way out, wanted to be taken away from everything that was suffocating her. He would be the man to help her, to make her realize that she was just like him. Tonight he would make that happen.

He stayed in the shadows and watched the party guests arrive. But only Abe knew there would be no wedding. He blended into the darkness with his black fatigues and dark boots. He didn't miss anything, and absorbed everything.

Alert. Prepared. Anticipating.

He took in the sound of the wind moving through the trees, of the tires from the approaching cars moving along the gravel driveway, and of the laughter and conversation from the people only feet away. He analyzed each syllable and took note of the minutest detail. When the last guest had entered the mansion and the valet had parked the final luxury car, Abe moved further into the shadows and around the back of the house. Security was stationed around the perimeter, but they didn't have the training he had. They didn't know the signs of a predator amongst them... when *he* was right in front of them.

Abe stopped in front of the large picture window that showed into the dining hall. A hundred guests sat at white cloth-covered tables and drank from their gold-gilded champagne flutes. But he didn't need to scan the room to know where Bethany was. She sat at the head of the table in the front of the room, dressed in an innocent and delicate white dress. The tiny white lights cast a plethora of gold and rainbows around her, and everything inside of him tightened.

He clenched his hands into fists at his sides and felt the darkness inside rise violently the longer he stared at her. He wanted her now, but he needed to be smart about this. Her long dark hair was piled high on her head and her delicate neck invoked images of him biting at her tender skin, leaving bruises and marks so he could see the proof of his ownership. He was hard, so fucking hard he could rival the strength of steel.

And then Abe trained his gaze on the man that threatened what Abe wanted. He was an abuser, a womanizer, and the man that used the façade of being noble and sophisticated to manipulate others. He was the one that planned on taking Bethany away from Abe, of using her in the most deplorable way and playing it off as what husbands did with their wives. Abe knew all about him, had watched him, learned his habits, and had stopped himself many times from taking matters into his own hands and ending the miserable bastard. Abe could say what he planned on doing was because of those reasons alone, but that would be a fucking lie.

He had originally planned on taking Bethany away from all of this solely because he wanted her. She would be his, *only* his, and anyone that thought of standing in his way would see firsthand exactly how deadly he was. And the main obstacle was her fiancé, Steven Michael St. Gerrard.

———

February 2014

"WHAT ARE YOU GOING TO DO?"

Bethany didn't respond right away, and lifted her gaze from the cappuccino in front of her to stare at Madison.

Her friend since grade school was just as prim and proper as every other person in Bethany's life. Madison held her focus on her phone, and although she had acted concerned about Bethany's situation, she seemed more concerned in texting her boyfriend, Blaine.

Bethany stared at her friend with the cream-colored cardigan wrapped around her shoulders, her taupe blouse, and her equally bland and neutral skirt. Madison was the epitome of the type of woman her father wanted *her* to be. But everyone in the restaurant was dressed in the same upper-class and snooty manner. Bethany looked down at herself and picked at her off-white cardigan. She hated that she was a sheep amongst the flock, but doing anything other than that would have had others look down on her. When she looked back at Madison she saw her friend now watching her.

"So what are you going to do?" Madison asked again as she grabbed her coffee. Bethany watched the droplets of condensation slide down the clear, smooth crystal, and knew that saying any more wouldn't solve this problem.

"There isn't anything that I can do. What choice do I have but to marry a man I don't love, and live this lie of a life?"

Madison shrugged. "You're being dramatic. You could have it much worse than becoming engaged to Steven. He is wealthy, a gentleman, and so very attractive. You could have been set to marry Marshall Booviaire."

"Marshall?"

"Yeah, you know that Frenchman Clarrisa Harshton married. He was like twice her age, wasn't nearly as wealthy as Steven, and he even smelled funny."

"Oh yeah, I completely forgot about Clarissa and him." Bethany reached for her tea and took a sip.

"So see, you could have it much worse."

Bethany didn't respond, didn't really know how to respond in fact. She honestly didn't even know why she had agreed to come to brunch with Madison or say anything to her. No, that wasn't true. She had maybe thought her friend, the one she had known her whole life, might be able to sympathize with her.

"You didn't go around telling anyone else that you don't want to marry Steven, did you?"

"I talked to my mother and father. My mom was more dismissive of the whole idea, and kept talking about what a good match he was. My father..." Just thinking about that conversation left a bad taste in her mouth. "He more or less cut the conversation off before it started." Even now she could hear her father's deep voice telling her that she owed them this, that they had gone through a lot of trouble ensuring she was to wed a prestigious "stud" such as Steven. And yes, he had used the word stud like she was some kind of breeding mare. "I never said I didn't want to marry Steven, Madison." *You've thought it every single day or every single second since you were told you'd be strapped with him.*

Madison gave her the look that said it was a bunch of

bullshit, and then exhaled loudly. "No, you didn't, but I know what you meant regardless." Madison leaned forward and rested her hands on the table. She rubbed her fingers along the pearl bracelet, and it was clear to Bethany that her mind was otherwise occupied. "You need to think about your family, your status, and not so much about what you would get from it."

Bethany stared at Madison, aghast. "Listen to yourself."

Madison leaned back in her seat and gave her a pinched expression. "And what should I be listening to?"

At twenty-two, they both knew what Bethany was talking about. They had lived the same life, gone to the same private school and the identical uptight parties, and knew that status and reputation were everything. "You know what I mean, Madison. What about marrying someone because you're in love and not because it will better the family, or for political reasons? What about not having to watch what you say, what you wear, and always having to act like you are living someone else's life?"

Madison made a scoffing noise, and instead of answering right away lifted her hand and snapped her fingers for the waiter's attention. A small man, with a perfectly-ironed black and white uniform, hands behind his back and nose in the air, stepped up to the table.

"Yes, Madame, how may I help you?"

"Please box up a dozen of these glazed scones."

The waiter nodded, turned to Bethany, and when she

shook her head that she didn't want anything he disappeared toward the back of the restaurant.

Madison was staring at her again, and then exhaled, overly dramatic. "Listen, I totally see where you are coming from. You think I want to be straddled with some random guy, especially if he is old as hell?" She shrugged. "But we were born into this life, and because of that we have to abide by certain rules and standards. You know that."

Bethany kept her mouth shut. She had been foolish to think expressing herself like this would have the desired effect. "Everything is just moving so fast. I've just barely graduated, hardly even started my life, and my father pulls this shit on me." She closed her eyes and scrubbed her hand over them.

"You just need to go with the flow. At least you are going to marry Steven. Just be grateful on that part."

"One of these days I might just leave, Madison."

Madison rolled her eyes. She picked up her napkin and dotted the edges of her mouth. "Who's being dramatic now? Besides, you and I both know you wouldn't just leave. What would you do for money? Work? Your father has all the connection, and leaving when you are all set to marry Steven would not only be disastrous, but also stupid. You'd lose everything."

What Madison didn't know, or failed to really understand, was that Bethany didn't care about money or power, or even about her social standing. She had gone to school to be a social worker, much to her father's distaste. But her father, Robert Maximus Sterling, didn't derive pleasure in things that helped him gain power, money, or increase his social standings. She had been born to the wrong family.

"Everything will be fine. You think people have to be madly in love to be married?" Madison flicked her hand between them. "I guarantee you'll be gushing about how wonderful it is to be married to Steven not long after the wedding."

"Doubtful."

"Let's go to Angelo's and get our nails done." Madison lifted her hand and stared at her already French manicured tips. And just like that, the conversation that had been very important to Bethany had ended as if it had never really begun.

Ten minutes later they left the restaurant, but Bethany wasn't in the mood to get her nails done. With her wedding only months away she was feeling the strain and stress of everything weighing down on her. The wedding planner took care of almost everything, but the most pressing issue was the fact she didn't know Steven. Being around him, speaking with him, even going on dates hadn't allowed her to even know who he was. He talked shop a lot, something she heard enough of when she was at home. But there was something underneath Steven's exterior, something that had the hairs on the back of her neck rising and her heart racing, but not in the good way.

It was like a sixth sense that rose up when he was around. She pushed the discomfort away, focused on her own life, and tried to tell herself that this would all work out in the end. Yes, she was an adult and made up her own mind when it concerned her life, but she was also frightened of what the future held. If things went downhill after the marriage would she be able to leave unscathed, and still have her family's support? The latter, she was sure, wouldn't be the case.

She climbed into her car, shut the door, and just sat there for several moments. What money she did have was courtesy of her father, and because she had just graduated it wasn't like she had a steady income. God, she didn't even have a job yet, and as much as her father tried to push her toward a profession that wouldn't have her "eating boxed dinners," she was tired of this regimen that controlled her entire life. She started the car and pulled out of the lot. Home didn't even sound welcoming or warm anymore—if it ever had at all.

For the next twenty minutes she left the city of Sinnerstown behind. The irony of living in a town that was named after the corrupt and disgusting things she had seen her father and their associates do, all for the name of bettering their families, was not lost on her. The gated entryway that led up to her family's estate loomed in front of her. She hadn't always felt this way, not to this extent, at least. But Bethany had always felt this sort of hollowness as she moved with the tide and did what was expected of her.

She had considered herself a "sheep" or a "doormat" and because of that hated herself more than anyone could have ever known. Once she typed in the security code the gates opened to allow her entrance. She drove up the long driveway, past the security stationed throughout the property, and pulled to a stop in front of the doors.

"You either need to go through with this, or shut the hell up. All you're doing is making yourself sick." Closing her eyes, she breathed in and out and took in the sounds around her: people speaking just a few feet away, the sound of shears clipping away at hedges around the perimeter of the house, and even water trickling into the pond from the fountain. When she opened her eyes and lifted her head she was staring at the man that made her feel uncomfortable. In fact, the way he watched her was what she noticed first.

Abe Sparrow had been hired to watch over her father, but he looked at her as if he could read every personal thought in her head. He was darkly handsome, in a kind of way that made her feel nervous. His black hair was cropped short and his equally dark eyes always seemed trained on his surroundings. She wasn't privy to her father's affairs, and didn't know the details and backgrounds of the security he hired.

But she had overheard talk that Abe was lethally trained, and not in the conventional way. She wasn't naïve enough to think that he didn't know how to kill a man with his bare hands and without remorse.

She was the one to break eye contact with him, but she still felt his gaze on her. Bethany grabbed her bag and climbed out, but she couldn't help herself. Her gaze lifted and locked with his once more. God, even from a distance he was big and imposing, and the dark clothing he wore didn't hide the fact that he was built like some kind of deadly machine.

"Bethany, sweetheart."

She gritted her teeth when she heard Steven's voice, and then saw his car parked a few feet away. Her thoughts had been so jumbled that she hadn't even realized he was at the house. When she looked back at where Abe had been standing, she saw that he was no longer there.

"We were just talking about you." Steven was right beside her now, and wrapped his arm around her shoulder.

A chill of discomfort filled her, but she forced a smile when she saw her father standing on the porch, watching them. "I didn't know you'd be home." She spoke to her father, and moved up the steps so she was right in front of him. Thank God Steven had let go of her, because his touch was akin to acid on her flesh.

"I leave this evening." He spoke around his cigar.

The sickening sweet stench of it surrounded her, but she held in her cough.

"Steven is going with me to close the Browne account."

She nodded, surprised that her father was bothering to tell her something work-related.

"In fact, Steven, you should just tell your fiancée now instead of waiting." Her father grinned, but it wasn't one of those loving, happy ones.

Bethany glanced at Steven, curious as to what would be so important that her father wanted her to know now.

"I've made partner, Bethany." Steven grinned, and before she knew what was happening, she was in his arms and he was kissing her. But the feel of his lips on hers was cold and not the least bit arousing. He pulled away, his grin right back on his face, and turned to look at her father. "Soon I'll be part of your family by marriage, and even closer by business."

Of course she didn't miss how he had classified the business as most important, because to men like Robert Sterling and Steven St. Gerrard, there was nothing more important than that.

———

Available Now: https://amzn.to/2Jl6BRk

ABOUT THE AUTHOR

Find Jenika at:

Instagram: Instagram.com/JenikaSnow
Goodreads: http://bit.ly/2FfW7AI
Amazon: http://amzn.to/2E9g3VV
Bookbub: http://bit.ly/2rAfVMm
Newsletter: http://bit.ly/2dkihXD

www.JenikaSnow.com
Jenika_Snow@yahoo.com

96894075R00130

Made in the USA
Columbia, SC
09 June 2018